PUSH the ENVELOPE

Felicia,
    Thanks for going
mile high with me.

ROCHELLE PAIGE

Dedication

Mitchell & Max –
Dream big.
Fight hard.
Make it happen.

prologue

FLOWERS…CHECK.

Chocolates…check.

Champagne chilled and ready to go…check.

Noise-canceling headphones so I didn't have to listen to whatever noises were going to float up from the rear cabin…check.

This was so totally not the normal pilot's checklist. When I talked to Dad over the summer about offering Mile High Club charter flights so we had some extra money coming in to cover my room and board at college, I had no idea how the idea would take off. I'd figured I would take a couple flights out each month so Dad wouldn't have to scrimp on anything so that I could live on campus. He really wanted me to get the whole college experience, especially since I had chosen to stay in town for school.

Who knew there were so many middle-aged housewives looking to spice up their marriages? I usually had three to four flights booked each week now. At a cool grand per booking, we made enough to cover my room and board and maintenance on the planes, and we even had money left over to pay off my student loans and to cover my tuition for my next two years. I guess they're right when the say sex sells!

Since the flights were offered in the evening, they didn't interfere with my classes. Dad wanted as little to do with this venture as possible. He had told me that this was my idea, and he expected me to run with it. Talking about anything connected to sex with his daughter wasn't really high on his list of things to do. I figured I was lucky that he was willing to let me use the Cherokee for the flights. I just had to make sure I booked them when I was able to be in the pilot's seat. The last thing I wanted to do was screw my grade point average over because I was skipping too many classes to pilot the flights I was only offering so I could pay for school in the first place.

Today's flight was due to depart in about thirty minutes, so the lucky couple should be here any minute now. I needed to get my butt in gear so I would be ready when they arrived. The plane was set up for their romantic rendezvous. I was dressed in my charter pilot gear of loose khaki pants and a Hewett Charters polo shirt. I'd pulled my long brown hair back in a low ponytail. This appearance seemed to help the wives feel more comfortable with the idea that their pilot was a twenty year-old girl. Add into the equation that I am passably attractive and I could have a problem on my hands with my paying customers. So I did what I could to make sure I presented myself as a capable pilot and nothing else.

I know it's crazy for some people to picture me piloting a plane, but I started flying with my dad before I ever got behind the wheel of a car. He lived to fly and taught me to love it as well. I had my permit when I was sixteen, earned my private license when I was seventeen, and got my professional license when I turned eighteen. Some days it felt like I spent more time during my life up in the air than I did on the ground.

Yet another reason Dad wanted me to live on campus this year— so I could hang out with girls and act my age. Dad and I had been two peas in a pod forever, and now he worried that I needed to have a normal life with girlfriends, parties, and boys. I admit that my upbringing wasn't exactly orthodox, but I was happy with the way things were. I just wished Dad would understand that.

Damn, it sounded to me like my housewife of the day had gone all out for this trip based on the click of her stilettos hitting the tarmac. I didn't understand how women could walk on shoes that looked like skyscrapers to me. Guess that was just the tomboy in me, much to my best friend's dismay. Time to get my head in the game so I didn't scare off the paying customers.

"Welcome to Hewett Charters," I greeted the middle-aged couple as they made their way towards me. "You must be Mr. and Mrs. Williams?"

"Yes, that's us," tittered the platinum-blond woman as her husband looked at me quizzically. I guessed that she hadn't used their real name in the hope that they could keep their trip private. She needn't have had that concern since I offered complete confidentiality.

"Thank you for booking your flight with us today," I said. "Everything is all set, and we can be in flight as soon as you are ready to go. Did you have any questions before we board?"

"Ummmm, are you our pilot?" asked Mr. Williams.

"Yes, I'm Alexa Hewett. Don't worry. You're safe with me. I've been doing private sightseeing tours for a couple years and have had my pilot's license for almost three years. I might be a little young, but I grew up with my dad in the cockpit of a plane. I can assure you that I am fully qualified to take you up," I answered.

"And how does this work exactly?" he questioned.

I couldn't help but smile at the question. It seemed that the wives always booked these flights, and the husbands always seemed uncertain once they got here. I even had flights where the husband had no idea that his wife had booked the tour with the sole purpose of getting it on mid-flight. The expressions on their faces when they saw the bed in the cabin were priceless. It kind of cracked me up since I always figured guys were less shy about sex. Which may still prove to be true since I hadn't seen a single guy yet turn down the opportunity offered by my special charter flights.

"If you will follow me this way, you can see how we've set the Cherokee up so that you will have plenty of room in the rear cabin. Once we are in flight, I will draw the privacy curtain and wear noise-canceling headphones during the flight. I will be able to communicate with the tower but won't be able to hear anything from the cabin. Any of your activities while on board will be as private as possible." They both nodded and looked at each other while blushing.

I walked the couple towards the plane, showed them the bed area we had fashioned by removing four of the seats, and asked them to sit in the rear-facing seats during takeoff for their safety. If the hot looks they were flashing each other as they buckled up were any indication, they were ready to go.

3

"Enjoy the refreshments, and I will let you know when it is safe to move about the cabin," I said as I got settled into the cockpit.

As I prepared for takeoff, I couldn't help but chuckle to myself about the irony of me helping couples to spice up their sex lives. I wasn't exactly qualified to do so except for piloting the plane. I couldn't really be described as very experienced in the bedroom. Yet, I have turned my beloved Cherokee into the equivalent of a by-the-hour hotel room.

Chapter 1

"HONEY, I'M HOME," I yelled out to my best friend Aubrey as I entered our suite. I was thrilled that she and I could be roomies when I made the switch to living on campus this year. The upside to the extra cash that came in with the mile high flights was that I could afford the brand new dorm that offered suites on campus. Blythe College had built the dorm in an effort to compete with the off-campus apartments. Our suite offered us our own bathroom, a common area, and two double bedrooms that my best friend and I shared with two other roommates. There were six suites on our floor, and we all shared a kitchen and entertainment area where we could hang out and watch television if we wanted.

I was excited to get into this dorm. It meant we could share a room without my dad harassing me about us living in each other's pockets. He wanted me to make new friends at school, and I was happy to have the compromise of two more roommates in the suite so he wouldn't try talking me into rooming with someone else. I couldn't begin to imagine living on campus without Aubrey at my side. We met on the first day of kindergarten and have been besties ever since.

I hadn't been excited about my first day of school and being away from my dad. I was a total mess when I got to the school that first morning, clinging to him like I would never see him again. It was crazy when you considered that I didn't usually spend all day with him anyway, but I was terrified of what would happen when he was away while I was at school. Separation anxiety didn't even begin to describe how I had felt that day.

Aubrey's mom was with her and quickly realized that my dad wasn't handling the situation very well. Luckily, Mrs. Silver stepped in to help us out by introducing me to her daughter, who glommed on to me instantly. Aubrey was the youngest of four with three older brothers and was thrilled to see another girl at school. She had been afraid that she would be stuck with boys all day long since her brothers' friends from school were boys.

She was a great distraction for me as she chattered away about what to expect since her brothers had all filled her in on the school experience. She was dressed up in a frilly dress, with ribbons pulling up her curly blond hair and shiny, buckled shoes on her feet. I didn't really know how to react to her and found myself swept away by her enthusiasm.

Sometimes I wonder if I hadn't been the first girl she met that day if our friendship would be the same. It was like I became her favorite pet, with her dragging me everywhere and trying to dress me up. Now that I think about it, things haven't really changed that much between us over the years.

It was great living with Aubrey, but I didn't think we had won the roommate lottery this time around. I hadn't taken much time to get to know the other duo that well. Faith and Natalie were way too high maintenance for my taste, and it seemed like they had only come to school to chase boys. We'd only lived together for less than three weeks and they had already hit six parties and skipped classes several mornings to sleep in. Only time would tell if we would be able to get along. Luckily, they were a good match with each other and seemed happy to hang out together. Aubrey got along with them fairly well. She definitely had more in common with them than I did. She could talk to them about fashion and boys, but I wasn't big on either topic.

"Lex! You're back just in time to get ready," Aubrey screamed, rushing towards me with her hair rolled up in curlers and makeup halfway done. It was a Friday night, so she was busy getting ready to head out for the night. Dance music was blaring to help her get into the right frame of mind. It looked like Faith and Natalie had already headed out for the night. Ugh… I wasn't really in the mood to head to a party tonight, but I knew Aubrey would have my ass if I said no.

I had been able to duck out the last two weekends, but it looked like my time was up.

The downside to having one bathroom—Friday and Saturday nights featured a mad rush as everyone fought for mirror space in the bathroom. Flat and curling irons hung from the outlets, hair products littered every surface, and makeup was scattered around. Four girls to one bathroom could cause some serious catfights around here.

"Here, put this on." Aubrey tossed a dress at me. A very small dress. A dress that should be a couple sizes smaller than mine, yet the tag matched my size. "I don't want to hear it. You are going out with us tonight, and you are going to look hot while doing it," Aubrey continued before I could even get a word in.

I held the dress up to my body as I glanced at the mirror. It couldn't be that bad, right? Shit, there was no way this was going to cover my ass all night long. "Really? This is what you want me to wear tonight? Are we going to a strip club?" I asked sarcastically.

"Nope. I am not taking any attitude from you tonight, Lex. I love you like my sister, so hear me when I say that you had better get your ass in gear so we can go party. We can sit here and argue about what you are going to wear tonight, but you know you'll just be wasting your breath because I'm going to win anyway. I would never let you go out looking like a total skank, so don't act like you think that I would." Aubrey glared at me from her startling blue eyes.

I recognized that look—the one that said, *You will do what I say, when I say it, if you know what's good for you.* She was right. It wasn't worth arguing over since she would win. She always did when she put her mind to it.

"Geesh, okay. I'll go get dressed. As long as you're styling me tonight, pick out shoes for me too. And you are also doing my hair and makeup," I answered.

"Duh," she snapped back at me. "Like I would trust you to do it yourself. Left to your own devices, you'd probably waste that gorgeous dress with a pair of flip flops, a ponytail, a swipe of mascara, and some chapstick. I think not!"

"Okay, okay. I surrender. It's not like I can argue with you when you're right. Snap to it, fairy godmother."

By the time we headed out the door, I didn't look like my usual self at all. The dress Aubrey had picked did cover my ass, hitting my legs mid-thigh. The rich purple color was one of my favorites, and the dress had a deep cowl neck that hinted at my cleavage without shoving it in everyone's faces. The girl certainly knew her stuff.

She let me out the door in ballet flats since she knew we'd end up in the emergency room if she made me wear heels. My hair was swept off my face and pulled into a barrette to one side with soft curls flowing down my back. I might be a bit of a tomboy, but I did love to keep my hair long. Dad always said that my hair reminded him of my mom, so I didn't have the heart to cut it too short.

My makeup was lightly done, but it accented my green eyes so they would draw attention. They were slightly slanted at the edges, kind of like cat's eyes. Aubrey always raved over them, often lamenting that it wasn't fair that my eyes were so cool when she had boring blue ones. I thought she was crazy since she had the whole blue-eyed blonde thing going on. Her Barbie-doll looks always drove the boys crazy, and I was sure tonight wasn't going to be any different.

Even though she went a little conservative on my look for tonight, Aubrey had gone the opposite direction with her own. Her bright red dress would draw attention by its color alone. Add in the fact that it clung to her like a second skin and was a couple inches shorter on her than mine and we were in for a riot tonight when the guys got a load of her. She'd picked out a pair of silver stilettos with rhinestones on them that added several inches to her height. She had topped it all off with smoky eyes and shiny red lipstick that I knew from experience wouldn't smudge all night long.

"What the hell, Aubrey? Are you on a mission to pick up a guy tonight or what? Aren't we way overdressed for a college party?

"Lex, sweetie. Trust me on this. We will fit right in tonight. I swung us an invite to the hottest party on campus, courtesy of my big bro. The Sig Chi's are throwing a 'welcome back to campus' party that is supposed to be epic. From what Faith and Natalie have said, the guys there are super hot. You know that means that the chicks are going to be dressed to impress tonight. There is no way I am going to this party without looking my best."

"A frat party? Really, Aubrey? I let you get me all dressed up so we could go to a frickin' frat party?" I was not happy. I didn't feel like partying tonight, and now I had to deal with a bunch of drunk frat boys trying to get in my panties all night long. "You are so lucky I love you right now. Or else I would be kicking your ass for putting me through this."

"Don't worry. Jackson will be there in case we run into any problems. You know my big bro will look out for you just as much as he does me, maybe even more. He's always been so protective of you. Which will work out great for me because you can distract him while I flirt with all his frat brothers!"

Aubrey wasn't joking when she suggested that I run interference for her with Jackson. That was part of why he and I had grown so close over the years. As the closest in age to her, Jackson was often tasked with running us around town and watching out for us at school. With us all on the same college campus now, he would definitely take his big brother role seriously. He had been bad enough in high school, scaring boys away from Aubrey left and right. I was surprised he was willing to get us into the party tonight.

"How did you get him to cough up an invite to the party tonight?" I asked.

"Well, I might have suggested that I was hoping you were finally ready to hit some parties tonight after working so hard all summer and settling into school the last couple weeks. And that I was worried you were never going to leave the room unless I had a really good reason to get you to go out tonight. And that if you knew we were going to a party he was going to be at, then you would feel more comfortable."

"So you basically guilted him into it then? Using me? And making me sound like a hopeless shut-in?"

Aubrey laughed. "Yup. Worked like a dream! He even said that Faith and Natalie could come too, so maybe I did lay it on a little thick."

Chapter 2

DAMN. AUBREY WASN'T kidding when she'd said that the Sigma Chi party was supposed to be epic. The house was packed with people, music was blaring, and drinks were flowing. Our IDs had been checked out the door, so we were stuck with lame under-21 hand stamps for the night. Not that it really mattered once we made it through the door, since Aubrey talked the first guy she saw into grabbing us two beers from the keg.

As we wandered through the downstairs area with our red Solo cups in hand, I had to admit that she was right when she'd said that we wouldn't be overdressed tonight. I could swear that I had the longest dress on, and that was with a hem a good two inches shorter than what I was normally comfortable in whenever Aubrey talked me into wearing a dress. Some of the outfits tonight showed more skin than bikinis with cover-ups did at the beach. And you'd think we were on the set of a music video with the way the girls were grinding against each other on the dance floor. I was so out of my element it wasn't even funny.

Aubrey was busy chatting up a totally hot redheaded guy when I noticed Jackson across the room. I tapped her on the shoulder and nodded my head in his direction so she would know where I was heading. I barely got a glance from her as she was busy flirting. That girl went through boys like water, with no particular type that appealed to her. She flitted from boyfriend to boyfriend, breaking hearts wherever we went.

Speaking of broken hearts, Jackson had a flock of girls around him tonight. I hated to interrupt, but his was the only other familiar face at the party I had seen so far. Faith and Natalie were nowhere to be found, and I highly doubted any of the friends I had made in class had been invited to this party.

Jackson glanced up as I approached the group of girls surrounding him. A wide smile broke across his face. With his curly blond hair tousled from running his hands through it and his eyes twinkling at me, I could understand why I was receiving death glares from his fan club. I had drawn his attention away from them.

"Alexa, you made it!" Jackson reached out to pull me over to him, wrapping me up in a bear hug. "Fuck, you clean up nicely. I think the last time I saw you in a dress was at graduation. And your dress then left a little more to the imagination. Did Aubrey have to tackle you to the floor and wrestle you into this one?"

Yup, those death stares were now hitting my back like laser beams. Add in the snarky little laughs and I was starting to get pissed off. Could they not tell that we were practically brother and sister? Geesh, catty bitches were guaranteed to drive me crazy. I kissed him on the cheek and kept an arm wrapped around his side just to put them in their place.

"Nah. She worked her guilt magic on me just like she did you to get the invites to the party. You know how she is."

"That I do, Lex. That I do. But she didn't really have to guilt me into making sure you guys got into the party. You know that I wasn't letting you go to your first official college party without being there." Jackson took a sip from his beer, glanced at the girls around us, and carried on the conversation like they weren't there. "Where did my sis run off to?"

"Oh, she's around here somewhere. She can't get into too much trouble since everyone knows she's your sister, right?"

"Ha! You know better than that. Aubrey doesn't need to find trouble—it finds her. Lucky for me, I planned ahead and asked a few of the guys to keep an eye on her tonight. Figured I would need reinforcements to make sure we make it through the night without my having to beat the shit out of anyone."

I couldn't deny that there was a real possibility that Jackson might get into a fight tonight, even if it wasn't because he was pulling Aubrey out of a situation she couldn't handle. He had a very short fuse and was quick to jump down someone's throat if he thought they'd fucked up. Over the years, Aubrey had certainly offered up several guys who got the shit kicked out of them by Jackson when they wouldn't leave her alone after she'd dumped them. It wasn't that she got into trouble often. It was just that her ex-boyfriends never seemed willing to let go.

"Aubrey doesn't have any ex-boyfriends that go to school here yet, so she shouldn't get into too much trouble," I reminded Jackson.

"But I am sure she is working on meeting her next ex, right?"

"Well, there was a guy that she was flirting with over there. He seemed nice enough. He had an under-twenty-one stamp, too, so I would guess he's a freshman or sophomore." I pointed over to Aubrey so he could see where she was at across the room.

"Good. I don't recognize him, and if he had a hand stamp then he isn't one of my frat brothers. I'd hate to have to kick a brother's ass later if things go south." Jackson finished off his beer. "Want another one?" he asked as he tapped his empty cup against mine.

I nodded, so we headed over to the keg to grab another drink. As we walked away, I could hear one of the girls whining Jackson's name. He just shook his head at her as he held on to my hand so he wouldn't lose me in the crowd.

"So Aubrey isn't the only one working on their next ex around here?" I asked Jackson.

"It wasn't like that with her. You know how girls can be. Sometimes they think things are more serious than they really are."

Aubrey wasn't the only one in her family who'd left a trail of broken hearts in their wake. The big difference between the two was that Aubrey jumped into relationships and then bailed when she got bored. Jackson never let it get that serious. There were always girls around—he just never called them his girlfriends. It had always surprised me how he treated the girls he'd slept with when he would kill a guy if he treated Aubrey or me the same way, but Jackson always told me that the girls he was with had known the score and had nobody to blame but themselves if they thought he'd been willing to give them something more.

12

When we made it over to the keg to grab another beer, my attention was drawn to the kitchen door. Just outside, an argument was taking place between a screaming girl and a super hot guy who stood staring at her with his arms crossed in front of his chest. The girl was gorgeous and dressed to the hilt. Her platinum blond hair was perfectly straight and her makeup expertly applied while her outfit had clearly set her back big bucks. Too bad for her that the attitude didn't appear to match the wrapping.

Holy crap. I could only see the guy she was yelling at from the side, but what I could see made me want more. There was something about him that pulled me like a magnet. He was a couple inches over six feet with dark brown hair that was spiked up a bit. His jeans clung to his tight ass and tapered down his long, muscular legs. He wore a bright blue polo shirt that stretched across his back each time he moved. He definitely worked out, but he was lean instead of bulky. Even with the girl yelling at him, he seemed so relaxed, like he didn't have a care in the world.

Jackson turned to hand me my cup and noticed where my attention was focused. "Shit! Who told Sasha about the party? Hold on a second while I make sure Drake doesn't need any help getting her to leave. Then we can check on Aubrey and head upstairs to my room to hang out. That way you can relax without pissing my sis off by heading back to the dorm this soon."

"Okay, sounds like a plan to me," I responded. It had been a long day between classes and my charter flight. I could use some extra rest. Besides, I didn't need to ogle one of Jackson's frat brothers who already had his hands full with women issues. That was just asking for trouble, even if he was smoking hot.

The girl stopped her tirade when she saw Jackson walking up. He could be very intimidating when he wanted to be. Jackson looked between the two of them, Drake shaking his head no and the girl taking a couple steps back. Dark, smoldering eyes met mine as Jackson talked to Drake. His gaze was so intense as he did a quick scan down my body, his eyes turning even darker as they lingered on my legs, which only served to piss off the blonde he had been arguing with moments before even more. She stomped off in a huff, leaving Drake and Jackson standing at the door.

They talked for a few more minutes while I waited. I couldn't hear what was being said as they spoke in hushed tones. Drake turned so he was facing me while they talked. He kept glancing my way as though he was having a hard time concentrating on his conversation with Jackson. He had a strong face with high cheekbones and full lips that made me think of kissing. Every once in a while, a dimple peeped out on the left side of his face, making him even more adorable.

He looked back at me again and smiled a sexy grin with one side of his mouth tilted up. Jackson shook his head, and Drake's body language changed completely. He wasn't the relaxed frat brother chatting with a friend anymore, but a man who looked like he was ready to strike out in anger. His fists clenched at his sides, and the cords of his neck stood out. Jackson reached out to him, but Drake took a step back and glared at me.

When Jackson came back over, he didn't offer to introduce us. I figured that meant he didn't trust Drake around me. With the death stare Drake was aiming my way, I didn't want him near me anyway. Then again, Jackson didn't really trust anyone around me since he seemed to think I wasn't capable of handling guys after the debacle with my ex-boyfriend in high school. As grateful as I was for him stepping in and ending the problem with Brad, I really wished he would get over the idea that I wasn't ready to date again. Sometimes it seemed like he felt so bad about introducing me to Brad that he would never be ready to see me with someone in my life again.

"Ready to hang out? Or do you want to join Aubrey?" Jackson asked.

"Ha, ha! Like that's even a question you need to ask me. You know I'd rather escape upstairs to hang out and get away from the madness of the party for a while without having Aubrey jump all over me for never going out. But don't you need to stay down here longer since it's your fraternity party?"

"Nope, the party's covered. My bros have everything under control. They knew I would bail early tonight," Jackson replied.

"And how many girls are going to want to kill me when they realize you left the party early because of me?" I asked, only half joking. I hadn't been on campus that much over the last two years other than to be at class or in the library, but the time I had spent hanging out with Jackson and Aubrey had shown me that most girls who were into Jackson liked hating me for my relationship with him. Nobody seemed to understand that we were like brother and sister, sometimes even more so than he and Aubrey appeared to be.

"If anyone has a problem with you, come to me. Nobody here has any say over what I do with my time—certainly not any of the chicks," Jackson said as we walked up the stairs after waving to Aubrey from across the room. "The only thing you need to worry about tonight is what movie you want to watch with me. I grabbed a few of your favorite action flicks. You can pick one and show me why you and your dad watch these so often."

Chapter 3

"UGH, MY HEAD," I heard Aubrey moan from under the covers. Jackson and I had hauled her home around three o'clock in the morning. "Why did you let me drink so much last night? I don't think I am going to be able to make it out of our room all day today."

"Let you? When have I ever let you do anything? You were on a roll last night. There was no stopping you and Mr. Hot Pants from chugging away. Not sure he's going to be the best boyfriend material for you if he's trying to get you drunk all the time."

"Why do you think every guy I hang out with has to be boyfriend material? Can't I just have a little fun every once in a while without getting too serious?" Aubrey snapped back at me.

"Well—" I started to reply before she quickly interrupted me.

"Okay, I know, I know. Odds are he'll end up being my next boyfriend. I get it. I date a lot. Nothing wrong with that. This is the age where we are supposed to date around, experiment a little. Besides, one of us has to do the boyfriend thing. When are you going to stop using my brother as a shield from every opportunity for you to meet guys? Don't think I didn't notice that you two escaped the party for hours last night to hang out."

Ouch. I thought I had gotten that one past her with all the drinking last night. "Hey, you wanted me to go to a party with you. I went. Just because I spent part of the night hanging out with Jackson doesn't mean I didn't have a good time. I did. The party was a little too much for me."

"You can totally make it up to me if you make the famous Hewett Hangover cure for me. I could really use some help this morning."

"I've got you covered. Let me run out to grab a few things from the store, and I will wake you back up as soon as it's ready. Get some more rest. I wouldn't want you to ruin a perfectly good day with a hangover," I said as I walked towards the door, snagging my keys off the dresser on my way.

"Love you, Lex," I heard Aubrey mumble tiredly.

I FOUND A parking spot for my beloved car, a cherry red Mini Cooper with a white racing stripe. My dad surprised me with it on my sixteenth birthday. The car seemed like an odd match for my personality since it was so girly, but nobody knew the inside story. We used to do movie night at least once a week, usually action movies since my dad couldn't stomach chick flicks. One of our favorites was The Italian Job, and I loved the part where they modified the Mini Coopers for a robbery. We must have watched that movie a dozen times together, and I always giggled at the thought of those tiny cars hauling gold bars away at top speeds. Now, whenever I drive my car, I am reminded of movie nights with him.

Damn, the grocery store was packed for a Saturday morning. I only needed to grab a couple things, but it looked like this wasn't going to be quick. I really hated shopping, even at the grocery store. It was just my luck that it would be so busy. And here I was, in my old ratty sweats I had worn to bed last night. At least I didn't have to worry about impressing anybody here. One advantage to growing up in a college town is that all us townies knew each other pretty well. Everyone had seen me looking a lot worse than this at least once in my life.

I grabbed a basket off the stack by the carts and darted towards the produce section to grab some bananas, strawberries, raspberries, and blueberries for the smoothies. My dad's famous hangover cure was pretty simple, but they seemed to work wonders. He always said that the almonds helped settle your stomach and the berries aided in detoxing the liver. Throw in a banana for extra potassium and you were good to go. I had made my fair share for him over the years when he'd hosted poker nights for his friends. He needed to be bright-eyed the morning after so he'd be safe to fly.

Once I had grabbed the fruit and almonds I needed, I headed over to the spices aisle to pick up some vanilla extract and cinnamon. I wasn't sure what all was stocked in the kitchen on our floor, so I needed to buy some just in case. As I rounded the corner of the aisle, I glanced into my basket, trying to decide if I should get some more ingredients so I could make smoothies for Faith and Natalie too. It would be a nice gesture and a chance to try to connect with them.

"Oomph!" I grunted as I walked into someone's back. "I am so sorry," I started to apologize. I lifted my gaze from my basket to the person I had knocked into and realized it was the guy from the party the night before. And then I quickly discovered that he was even hotter close up. It sure didn't hurt that he was dressed in pressed khakis and another polo shirt—dark green this time. And here I was, dressed like a homeless person.

He had turned towards me while I was lost in thought and his hands wrapped around my arms to help steady me. His dark brown eyes twinkled at me as he smiled in response to my apology. He smirked at me with a half-grin that showed off the dimple in his left cheek.

"No problem. I was kind of hogging the aisle while I figured out which way to go to find greeting cards," he said.

"Oh, you can find those across the aisle a few rows that way," I offered while pointing in the direction of the card aisle. His hands felt like they were burning through my clothes as they gripped my arms. I stared at his full lips as I spoke. It was so hard to pull my gaze away from his lips—they just seemed to be begging for a kiss.

"Thanks. I know this sounds like a bad pick-up line, but don't I know you from somewhere? I'm Drake Bennett," he asked.

"What? Um, yeah, you do. I was at the Sig Chi party last night. I think you know Jackson? He's—" I started to respond, stopping when his hands dropped from my arms abruptly and his eyes lost the warmth they had only moments ago. What the hell was up with that? He and Jackson had looked friendly enough last night.

"Right. I remember. Better grab that card. See you around," Drake offered as he walked away. Well, so much for chatting up the hot guy at the grocery store. Funny, right? Like he would ever even flirt back. He was way out of my league, even when I looked my best like last night. Looking like I did today, I was surprised he even spoke to me at all. I could be such an idiot sometimes.

I grabbed the rest of the supplies I need and headed to the checkout. My phone rang, and my dad's photo flashed across the screen.

"Hey, Dad. What's up?" I answered.

"Honey, I was wondering if you wanted to grab some extra hours co-piloting the Lear this weekend. I booked a last-minute charter to the Greenwich, Connecticut. Want to meet me at the airport?" he asked.

"Absolutely! I need more hours on the Lear. And I'd love to see you, too. I can only do it if I make it back in time for my first class on Monday morning." I handed some cash over to the cashier as I spoke with my dad. I needed to run back to the dorm to clean up and change clothes, whip up the smoothies for the girls, and head over to meet my dad.

"I wouldn't ask you to join me if I thought it meant you would have to skip classes. School comes first, not flying. You know the rules, sweetie. We don't take off for another two hours. Meet me in ninety minutes?"

"I'll be there, Dad. Thanks for asking me to join you," I answered before climbing into my car to go back home.

Aubrey was passed out in bed when I got back to the dorm. I hadn't heard a peep from the other side of the suite, so I decided that Faith and Natalie must still be sleeping also. I figured I should have enough time to get ready before I made the smoothies and woke everyone up.

I loved having the bathroom all to myself, so weekend mornings were my favorite. I could linger in the shower without worrying about anyone else barging in on me. As I washed my hair with my favorite coconut lime shampoo, I couldn't help but think of Drake. I had bumped into him twice in less than twelve hours, and both times I'd felt a chemistry like I had never experienced before. The way he had first looked at me at the party and held on to my arms when I bumped into him at the grocery store made me think he might have felt it, too. But then he'd been so cold to me. It was just so confusing. He didn't even really know me. Why would he be angry with me?

I just didn't understand the male mind. Brad had been my only boyfriend, and I thought I knew him until things had gone south. We had dated for three years, and everyone thought we would end up getting married and having kids. Including me. When Jackson walked in on Brad cheating on me at a college party his freshman year, things got ugly fast. Jackson kicked his ass then and there and told him to never speak to me again. He was the one who'd told me what had happened, with Aubrey by my side through the whole ordeal.

I was so hurt and didn't know how to react. Everyone heard about what had happened because of the fight. The pitying looks at school were tough enough to bear. Then when Brad decided that he wanted me back and didn't care if he had to fight Jackson to accomplish his goal, things got even worse. Flowers showed up on my doorstep regularly. Text messages and missed calls came all the time. I tried to avoid Brad and was pretty successful at it until he started showing up everywhere I went. I wasn't sure how he knew where I would be, and it freaked me out. My dad talked to the chief of police about getting a restraining order, but I worried that it would push him over the edge. The boy I had fallen in love with had disappeared, and Brad became someone I hardly recognized.

Jackson and Brad had been friends throughout high school and had pledged Sigma Chi together. Their fight had caused some issues at the frat house, with most of the guys siding with Jackson since he was a legacy. When they found out that Brad had resorted to stalking me, Jackson pushed for him to be kicked out of the fraternity and had the support of a lot of influential alumni due to his family connections behind him.

When the chief of police went to his parents, they'd refused to believe that things had gotten that bad. They wouldn't intervene, so Aubrey and Jackson's dad did. He owned the local bank, which held the mortgage on their house. I wasn't supposed to know that he'd visited Brad's parents and told them that they needed to fix this or he was going to call in their loan. I'd heard my dad talking about it on the phone after Brad had transferred to a school out West. He didn't want to go, but his parents knew that they had to act fast or things were going to get bad for them. The Silvers had a lot of influence in town and had made it clear that they wouldn't mind using it on my behalf.

Brad's leaving was a godsend to me. I'd been able to finish high school without worrying about seeing him in town and move on with my life without him in it. What I hadn't been able to do was feel comfortable enough to date other guys. What happened with Brad had added some serious trust issues to my abandonment issues. Not a good mixture for teenage dating. I focused on school and flying and forgot about boys for a while. And when the time came for me to pick a college, it made sense for me to attend Blythe but stay at home with my dad. Until he'd decided that I needed to spread my wings and could only do that while living on campus. Brad hadn't been a problem for more than two years, and I didn't have an excuse to stay home any longer.

Did that mean I was ready to date again, too? If my reaction to meeting Drake was any indication, then the answer was a resounding yes. With his hands on my arms and his gorgeous brown eyes gazing into mine, all I had wanted to do was kiss his delectable lips. His little smirk had made me want to bite down on his lower lip to punish him for being so damn cocky. But then he'd seemed icy to me. I was better off not fantasizing about some guy who'd managed to tie me up in knots inside after a few sentences of conversation. My taste in guys sucked!

The bathroom door flew open, interrupting my line of thought. "Lex, I thought you were going to fix me up a Hewett Hangover Smoothie?" Aubrey whined at me.

"I am. Just give me a second to finish up in here. Dad called and wants me to join him on a quick charter to the East Coast this weekend. Can you throw a change of clothes and my Econ book into a bag for me?" I asked.

"As long as you promise to fix me up as soon as you are out of the shower. My head is killing me, and I need to get some studying done so I can party with Faith and Natalie tonight since you are abandoning me again!"

"Yeah, yeah, yeah. I know. I suck as a best friend. Sorry I have to bail on you tonight. Maybe we could do a movie night sometime this week?" I offered.

"Yay! But I get to pick the movie. No action movies! Chick flicks only, got it?" Aubrey replied as she walked out of the bathroom. I didn't know which was worse—the idea of going to another party with her or being stuck watching some dumb movie she picked out. *The things we do for our friends.*

By the time I had gotten ready to go, all three girls were sitting in the common area, waiting on me to make them smoothies. "Hey," I greeted everyone, and they nodded their heads at me and went on gossiping about the party last night.

"Did you hear what happened with Drake and Sasha last night?" Natalie asked. I almost nodded my head before I realized she wasn't speaking to me. Normally I would have no idea what she was talking about, but I was the only person in the room who had seen Sasha practically get kicked out of the party.

"No, what happened?" Faith replied as she leaned forward to catch everything Natalie had to say.

"I heard that Sasha showed up at the party, without being invited, because she'd assumed that Drake wanted her there. I don't know why she thought she was so special. Word around campus is that he never invites girls over to the house—ever. And certainly not for a party," Natalie gossiped. "And that when she showed up, he pulled her through the house and to the back door so he could make it clear to her that he didn't want her there. Supposedly, she freaked out and he had to force her out of the house."

"He did not force her out of the house," I chimed in before I realized what I was saying. Three sets of eyes swiveled towards me, shocked that I had something to offer to this conversation.

"I heard it from a very reliable source, Alexa. Sasha told her best friend what happened, and she told me directly," Natalie huffed at me. "How would you know any differently? I didn't think you even knew Drake or Sasha."

"Well, I don't exactly know them, but I was in the kitchen when they were arguing and she left the house."

"What were you doing in the Sigma Chi kitchen last night?" Faith asked me. "We didn't see you at the party at all. I thought you didn't make it there."

"I went to the party with Aubrey. I didn't stay downstairs that long. Maybe that's why you didn't see me? Anyway, when Jackson and I went to grab another drink before heading upstairs, we ran into Drake and Sasha arguing at the back door. Jackson talked with them, and she walked off in a tizzy over something. Nobody forced her to leave, but they definitely made it clear that she wasn't welcome."

"And what happened next? I can't believe you didn't tell me first thing this morning that you met Drake Bennett last night, Lex! Best friends are supposed to share stuff like that," Aubrey shrieked at me while Natalie and Faith nodded their heads in support.

"Nothing happened, Aubrey. Jackson only talked to the guy for a couple minutes, and he didn't introduce us. So, I didn't really meet him last night. I just kinda observed him from afar," I responded.

"How could you waste a golden opportunity like that?" gasped Faith. "Drake Bennett is the hottest guy on campus. Every girl wants to meet him. And you were in the same room with him and didn't make sure that Jackson told him who you are? You are crazy!"

"Nah, she's not crazy. She probably didn't even notice how hot he is. Lex, you need to pull your head out of your ass and start living again! If someone as sexy as Drake doesn't even capture your attention the teensiest bit, then I am seriously worried about you," Aubrey wagged her finger at me, and I started to blush in response.

Damn my fair skin.

"Wait a second! You did notice him, didn't you? I see that look. You've finally noticed another guy! Yay! So why didn't you say anything to him? Oh, crap. You were with Jackson. No way could you ask him to introduce you after everything that happened the last time he introduced you to a guy. Don't worry though. We will just have to make sure you have another chance," Aubrey rambled on. Great, now I was going to have to admit to seeing him again in the grocery store.

"Yeah, I don't think that's gonna happen. I already saw him again this morning at the grocery store. And you saw what I looked like when I left this morning. I bumped into him, he seemed nice, and then he was super icy to me. I don't think the third time will be the charm."

I quickly finished making their smoothies so I could get out of there. I really didn't want to get the third degree about some guy I was never going to date anyway.

"Here you go! This should help with the hangovers. I need to head out if I am going to make it to the terminal in time. See you guys on Monday." I grabbed my backpack off the floor near the door and peeked inside. "Thanks for throwing my stuff together, Aubrey. I appreciate it."

"Don't think that this conversation is over, Lex. We will talk about this later," Aubrey threatened.

Chapter 4

I PARKED THE Mini Cooper in my parking spot at the terminal. I rubbed my hands together in excitement as I thought about the upcoming flight. It wasn't often that I was able to get extra hours in the Lear since Dad used it for most of his business charter flights. I couldn't wait to get up in the air today.

As I headed towards the hanger, I could see my dad running over his checklist outside the plane. We had both picked the same dark purple polo shirt to wear today—my favorite color. I knew Dad wore it because he knew I loved when he wore his. He had let me pick the colors out on the last order of logo shirts, and he hadn't been too excited when he saw the purple ones, saying it was a little too feminine for him. Yet he still wore it because he liked making me happy.

"Hey, Dad. Great minds think alike, eh?" I gestured towards our shirts. He snorted in response to my teasing and reached out to give me a big bear hug.

"Alexa! Since I can claim half of your great mind, it only makes sense that we think alike. Right, sweetie?"

"Makes sense to me. Anything I can do to help get ready for the flight?"

"Yeah, could you make sure there are drinks and snacks in the cabin? We only have one passenger today, so we only need a few things available."

"Sure, Dad. Should I fluff a pillow and grab a blanket while I'm at it?"

"Alexa Marie, you know that our passengers pay for comfort and convenience. I know it's a pain to cater to them sometimes, but that doesn't mean you need to get sassy with me."

"Sorry, Dad. I'll can the attitude. I promise."

"Good, because he will be here any minute, and I want everything ready to go before he gets here. His dad is paying us good money to make sure his son makes it to some big party tonight." Dad smiled back at me, letting me know that he didn't really mind my attitude all that much.

As I worked to get everything set up in the cabin of the Lear, I could hear my dad talking to someone in the hangar. Sounded like our passenger was here a little bit early. As I leaned over, peering into the fridge to make sure we had a selection of beverages, I could hear footsteps climbing the stairs onto the plane.

"Well hello. I didn't realize the view would be this good or I would have had my dad charter all my flights through Mr. Hewett," I heard a husky voice murmur at me. I stood and twirled around, coming face to face with none other than Drake Bennett. Dammit! Three times now in twenty-four hours. Really?

"Drake," I gasped at him. His eyes were directed at where my ass had been moments before, but he raised them to look at my face now. And yet again, there went that molten gaze turning to ice when he realized who I was. Seriously, what had I done to offend this guy?

"Wow! Didn't see that coming. Does Jackson know that you're a stewardess? I can't imagine that he's cool with how often you must get hit on when you hang around horny businessmen all day, bending over like that."

"Wait, what? Why would Jackson care if I was a stewardess? Which I'm not, by the way."

"Right, sorry. I should have said flight attendant. Let me guess, you met Jackson because of the job. I almost forgot that he was the one who'd suggested this charter line to me. Guess he doesn't mind how often you get leered at since he hasn't talked you out of the job."

"Hey! First of all, Jackson would never try to talk me out of a job. He isn't like that. And secondly—"

"Yeah, you say that now. But you must not know him as well as I do. Your relationship with Jackson and your job choice really aren't any of my business. Let's just forget we've met before and carry on with this flight so I can get home for my mom's birthday party."

The nerve of this guy! He really was a total douche. Just the reminder I needed never to trust my hormones again. Geesh! Before I could respond, my dad climbed aboard and glanced over at us. He raised an eyebrow at me in inquiry, probably wondering why I was standing there, glaring at our passenger.

"Alexa, is everything all set for Mr. Bennett in the cabin?" he asked.

"Yes, Dad. He should be fine. Why don't you have a seat, Mr. Bennett?" I asked Drake in a sweet tone of voice. His head swiveled back towards me when I said Dad. Looked like that had surprised him. *Just wait for the next shocker. Flight attendant, my ass.* Not that I have anything against them, but I hadn't spent years training to be a pilot for some asshole to pass judgment on me for no reason at all.

"Why don't you go ahead and get settled in the cockpit?" Dad asked me. He recognized that sweet tone of voice of mine and knew I was pissed about something. He might not know what had happened, but he knew me well enough to know it was best to remove me from the situation.

"Sure, Dad. I'll see you up there."

"Cockpit? She doesn't need to be up there with you during the flight. She's welcome to stay back here with me instead. I'm sure it would be more comfortable for Alexa," Drake offered.

"Well, that might make co-piloting the plane a little difficult," my dad responded. Damn, I really wished I could have seen the look on Drake's face at that news. I couldn't help myself as I glanced back over my shoulder. Yep, that was a look of total shock. His jaw had dropped and he was looking at me like he couldn't believe what he had just heard. Served him right for making assumptions. I deliberately left the cockpit door open so I could eavesdrop on their conversation.

"I'm sorry, sir. Did you say she's your co-pilot?"

"I sure did. And she's a damn good one. Trained her myself. I'm lucky that my daughter shares my interest in aviation." I heard the air of satisfaction in my dad's tone as he replied. There wasn't much he liked more than the opportunity to brag about my flying. "Now, you'd better buckle up so we can depart on time. We should have a tailwind on the flight out, so I expect that we'll land in less than two hours."

"Yeah, okay. Thanks. I do need to make it to Greenwich on time or else I'll be late for my mom's birthday party. Last thing I want to do is piss her off." That explained our morning run-in at the store. He had been buying a card for his mom.

"Anything you'd care to explain to me?" I heard my dad ask from behind me as he entered the cockpit.

"Nothing much, Dad. Just someone I met through Jackson. He's one of his frat brothers," I replied.

Dad looked at me quizzically. I could practically see the wheels turning in his head. "Seemed like there was more to it than that when I walked in."

"Nah, he just mistook me for a flight attendant and got my back up a bit. Nothing to worry about, Dad." I eased his concerns as we went through the pre-flight checklist.

"That's not usually enough to light your fuse. But if that's the story you're sticking with, I'll let it be for now. We've got bigger fish to fry at the moment. Let's hit the air, sweetie." Dad winked at me and then focused on our takeoff.

Everything went well with the flight, and we landed in Greenwich right ahead of schedule. I let my dad take care of our passenger, in the hope that I could avoid seeing him again until we left for home tomorrow. There was just something about Drake that pulled me in, even as he pushed me away.

When I deplaned, I expected him to already be gone. I was surprised to hear his husky voice from behind me as I hefted my bag onto my shoulder. "Alexa, I'm glad I was able to catch you before I had to leave."

I turned to look at him as he was speaking. His dark eyes gleamed as he gazed at me. "You are?" I asked.

Drake nodded his head at my question. "Yeah. I wanted to apologize for earlier. I know I acted like a jerk. Jackson's my frat brother, and he would be pissed if he knew how I treated you before." He grinned at me as he was explaining, his lips turned up on one side in a sexy little smirk.

"Yeah, I don't think so. I'm pretty sure that Jackson would find you thinking that I am a flight attendant pretty hilarious, actually." I wanted to reach out and smooth a lock of his black hair as it flopped over his forehead when he shook his head.

"You really think so? 'Cause I haven't seen him find very much of anything that funny when it comes to his girls," Drake replied.

"Jackson can be protective, but he also has a good sense of humor. Trust me. He takes great enjoyment in teasing me all the time." I smiled at Drake, thinking that it was nice to be able to talk to him without sounding like a complete idiot.

Drake's deep chuckle in response sent shivers down my spine. "Are you and your dad set for somewhere to stay while you're here? If not, you guys can head to my parents' house with me for the night."

"Aren't your parents hosting a party this weekend and that's why you had to fly out?" I asked, confused as to why he was being so nice all of the sudden. His mood swings were bound to give me whiplash.

He nodded, his eyes twinkling with humor. "Yes, but there's plenty of room at their place. I'm sure you and your dad could bunk down in the pool house. It might be easier since I'm not sure what time I will be ready to leave tomorrow, and I'd feel better if I could tell Jackson that you were covered for the night. Your dad's here to chaperone, so it's not like he'll think anything is going on between us."

"Why would Jackson think that we'd need a chaperone to stay at your parents' house for one night? He's protective, but he's not that bad," I answered.

"Hey, I just don't want there to be any confusion on his part. He's my frat brother, and I feel like we're becoming good friends. I don't want to step on his toes at all here." Drake crossed his arms over his chest, and it felt like he was putting up a wall between us even as we were talking.

"Well, I am sure he would appreciate it, but he knows I'm a big girl and can take care of myself. It's not like he keeps me on a leash or anything."

Drake snorted in response, his smirk turning into a full-out smile. God, he was even more gorgeous when he smiled at me. "You'd know better than I would about that, wouldn't you? From what I've heard, a leash doesn't sound too far-fetched. A shame he found you first."

What the hell had he just said? Something about me, a leash, and Jackson? I must have lost track of this conversation somewhere. I could feel the blush burning its way up my neck and into my cheeks as I started to get royally pissed off. "Whoa, hold up a second there. What in the hell type of relationship do you think I have with Jackson anyway? 'Cause I gotta tell you, the closest he and I have gotten to a leash would be walking his mom's dog."

"He takes you to his mom's house?" Drake asked. Apparently, he couldn't feel the laser beams my eyes were shooting at him. He didn't seem to be quaking in fear since his damn lips were still smirking at me. Even angry, I wanted to lean over and bite his bottom lip. Damn it!

"Yeah, why wouldn't he? It's not like I even need an invitation from him since I've known his mom even longer than I've known him. And asking me a dumb-ass question isn't answering mine!"

"Language," Drake growled at me. Now he was correcting my language? In the middle of an argument? When he doesn't even really know me? You've got to be fucking kidding me!

"Stop right there! I get that you're hot. I am sure lots of girls will put up with your crap because they want to be with you. But that's not me. First of all, you have no right to tell me how I can and cannot speak. Second of all, the only reason I am swearing in the first place is because you are being an A-S-S. There. Is it better for you that I spelled it instead of just saying it?" I held my hand up as he started to answer me. "No, I am not done yet. I don't know what you think you know about me, but the only thing you do need to know is that I will not put up with you judging me. You got that?"

Drake's head went back as he howled with laughter. I started to storm off to look for my dad so we could head out, but Drake's hand gripped mine as I swung away from him. He held on tight as he pulled me toward him.

"Alexa, babe. Didn't mean to set you off. I jumped to a conclusion when we met. One that was clearly as wrong as thinking you were the flight attendant when I got on the plane today. I don't often find myself in this position, but will you please accept my apology? Again?" His finger rubbed the skin on my palm as he looked into my eyes. "I'd really like it if you would come with me to my parents' house. I want the chance to explain."

"That's not necessary. I'm sure my dad booked a hotel for us." I shook my head and tried to pull my hand away.

"Alexa, don't be hasty," my dad said from behind me. His eyes were glued to Drake's hand over mine. "I thought I taught you better than that. Never look a gift horse in the mouth. Besides, it will give me a chance to get to know Drake here."

"Yeah, Alexa. Don't you want your dad to get to know me?" Drake asked. He didn't let go of my hand. Instead, he pulled me towards the limousine waiting outside the hangar. A guest house, a charter flight for the weekend, and a limousine. Who was this guy?

My dad followed behind with our bags. Crap. I just couldn't see any easy way out of this. And now I could expect a million questions from my dad about Drake, too.

Chapter 5

LUCKILY, THE CAR ride from the airport to Drake's parents' house was only supposed to be twenty minutes. He and my dad seemed to get along very well. They mostly talked about sports, and I learned that Drake was attending Blythe College mainly due to the rugby team. Drake explained that most colleges offered rugby as a club sport, but he'd transferred this year when his dad learned that Blythe had decided to go the varsity sport route. He'd thought it would improve Drake's odds for making the Eagles, the US national rugby union sevens team. The Eagles were going to represent the US in the Summer Olympics in 2016, and his dad had high hopes that he would have the chance at a gold medal.

He kept possession of my hand all the way there as he argued the merits of adding new Olympic sports. My dad was old-school and didn't think that activities like trampoline should be recognized as a sport. The conversation didn't get too heated since he supported the idea of rugby as an Olympic sport, saying it was a real sport unlike badminton. But my body was burning up as Drake continued to rub his thumb across my palm and entwine my fingers with his. Every once in a while, his thumb would stroke between my fingers. Goose bumps pebbled across my skin each time his thumb moved. I struggled not to visibly shiver in reaction as I didn't want him to know how much his touch affected me.

I stared out the window the whole time, wondering what was happening. Why the sudden interest in me after being so cold earlier? Was he bipolar or something? Our chemistry might have been through the roof, but I wasn't sure it was worth the bother. I couldn't really trust a guy who didn't seem to know what he wanted, especially when girls must chase after him all the time. The last thing I needed was a repeat experience of the cheating boyfriend scenario, not that I thought we'd end up as boyfriend and girlfriend or anything. My mind just kept going around and around in circles.

I could feel Drake's gaze on me, practically burning a hole in the back of my head. My dad was accustomed to my occasional brain-dead moments when I would daydream and left me to my thoughts without thinking twice. Drake's hand squeezed mine as he tried to get my attention. We had turned onto a winding drive, lined by tall trees.

"Alexa, we're here," Drake said as we pulled up to a palatial farmhouse. This wasn't a house—it was a country estate. And I hadn't packed to see anything other than the inside of a hotel room, a couple local eateries with my dad, and the hotel swimming pool. Great. Another chance for me to look as unappealing as possible in front of Drake.

"Yeah, I kinda figured that one out myself when we pulled up to the house. Anything you forgot to mention about your parents, Drake?" I asked. Even though he could make me melt with the mere stroke of a finger against my skin, I was still pissed about what he had said earlier and wasn't looking forward to meeting his parents while feeling woefully unprepared.

"We didn't really have time to discuss much of anything. Did we, Alexa? I promise, you will love them. My mom will be excited to meet someone from school, and my sister will be thrilled to have another girl around the place for the day. You'll be like a surprise present for them."

My dad cleared his throat from behind us, reminding me that I kept forgetting he was here whenever Drake looked at me. Not a good sign at all. "Well, then I hope they think my dad's a present, too."

"Alexa, don't be so worried. Drake's father had offered to let me stay here when he booked the flight. I told him it would depend upon if I flew Drake up by myself or not. So we've both been invited to stay."

"Dad! You never said anything about staying here when you

asked me to come with you on the trip." I glared at my dad since I probably would have packed a little differently if I had known that we would be around people while we waited for the return flight home. Not that my dad would understand—his packing would be the same no matter where we went or what we did.

"Sorry, honey. Didn't think I'd take him up on the offer if you were with me. Figured you'd want to stay closer to town and explore a bit. But since you and Drake know each other, this makes more sense. Don't you think?" His tone of voice let me know that I shouldn't argue and reminded me that my dad was going to have lots of questions for me when we were alone.

"See. Nothing to worry about, babe. My dad already invited you, and you didn't even know it! I'm sure my mom has prepped the pool house just in case it was needed." Drake started walking around to the back of the house. "Let me get you settled in, and then I'll go find my parents to let them know you are here."

I gawked a bit at the Olympic-sized pool that was surrounded by slate tiles. The pool house was a two-story white structure that was a good three to four times bigger than the size of my suite at school.

"There are two bedrooms upstairs, so you'll have plenty of space. There's one bathroom upstairs and a bathroom with a walk-in shower downstairs." Drake opened the door to the pool house. We walked inside, straight into a living area with a big-screen television and a small kitchen off to the side. The decor was very masculine, and the place smelled like Drake, a woodsy scent with a hint of leather.

"Does anyone usually stay here?" I asked.

"Me. I like a little bit of privacy if I'm going to be here for any length of time, but I'll just use my rooms in the main house while we're here tonight."

"Sorry to displace you," my dad responded.

"No problem, sir. I'm glad you decided to stay with us instead of at a hotel in town. It will give me a chance to hang out with Alexa."

"Yes, I'm clear on the fact that you'd like to spend some time with my daughter. But how about you let go of her hand for now, son. I'm sure your parents are excited to see you. You should probably head on up and let them know you're here. We'll get ourselves settled." My dad glanced at Drake's hand, making it clear that he hadn't missed anything that had happened over the last half hour.

"Right. I'll try to come back before the party starts. I'm sure my mom will want both of you to join us tonight if you'd like," Drake offered.

"I think I'll be fine down here. I brought my book with me, and I can probably catch some college football on the big-screen down here. Alexa, you want to hang out with your good ol' dad?"

"Yes, yes I do! Thank you very much for the invitation, Drake, but I wouldn't feel right crashing your mom's birthday party. Besides, I didn't pack anything that would be appropriate anyway. Go spend some time with your family, and you can find me in the morning so we can finish that conversation from earlier."

Drake leaned over and lightly kissed my cheek, whispering in my ear. "We'll just see about that."

As Drake left us alone, my dad turned to me. "I thought you said Drake was just one of Jackson's frat brothers. Looked to me like he's something more than that."

"I don't know what to tell you, Dad. I met him last night while I was at a party with Jackson. Saw him again this morning at the grocery store, too. I barely know the guy."

"It certainly seems like he wants to get to know you. He seems nice enough, but be careful, sweetie. I'd hate to have to hurt him and lose his dad's business if he breaks your heart. But a dad's gotta do what a dad's gotta do, right?"

"Geesh, Dad! You're already threatening to beat him up if he hurts me?" I walked over to my dad to give him a big hug. "You really are the best dad ever, so you don't need to run around threatening guys who seem the least bit interested in your daughter just to prove yourself to me."

"You're fooling yourself if you think that boy is only a little bit interested, Alexa Marie."

"If you say so. Now I'm gonna head upstairs to get settled in and maybe get some studying done."

I was able to get one of my papers done before I heard a knock on the door downstairs. I hadn't heard a peep out of my dad in hours. Odds were that he'd fallen asleep watching football. I ran down the steps so I could answer the door before he woke up.

"Hello," said the gorgeous brunette at the door in greeting. Her baby face led me to believe that she was a couple years younger than I was, but her clothing made me reconsider her age. Her outfit consisted of skintight, dark blue jeans that looked like they had been custom made for her tucked into knee-high brown leather boots and an oversized, dark green cable-knit sweater that slipped slightly off her shoulder. She was carrying a dry cleaner's bag in one hand and a Louboutin shoe box in the other. "You must be Alexa. I'm Drake's sister, Drea. But you can call me your fairy godmother!"

"Would that make me Cinderella? If so, I'm missing the wicked stepmother and sisters."

"Ah, yes, but wouldn't my brother make a perfect Prince Charming?" Drea giggled, and her eyes twinkled with laughter. I could definitely see the resemblance with her brother. Her parents had passed along very good genes to their children.

"I'm not sure that I'd use the word charming to describe your brother. He hasn't lived up to the title with me yet."

"Darn! Maybe you'll change your mind when I tell you that he let me know that you didn't know about the party when you flew up here with him. He's so bad like that, never remembers to tell me anything. Anyway, he asked if I could find you a few things so you would feel more comfortable joining us tonight."

"There wasn't any reason for me to know about the party, so Drake didn't forget to tell me." I spoke quickly, trying to get a word in edgewise while Drea took a breath.

"No reason? You don't need a reason to come to my mom's party. You're Drake's friend from school. That's enough. I'd be absolutely crushed thinking of you stuck in the pool house while we're all having fun. Besides, I'd love to show you off to everyone. Nobody will believe me for a second if I say that Drake has a girlfriend here with him from school."

"I am not his girlfriend! I hardly even know your brother. We just met last night," I disagreed.

"Really? Interesting. My brother isn't exactly known for going out of his way for girls. He met you last night and brought you here today? And he had me find you an outfit for mom's party. Lucky for him he thought we were about the same size. And one of my friends is your shoe size, so I didn't have to work too hard on the outfit. Anyway, big bro is smitten! I cannot wait to get to know you better."

Drake strolled up the sidewalk and rested his hand on his sister's shoulder. "Don't give away all of my secrets at once, Drea. Alexa is bound to keep me on my toes without any help from you." He reached around her to take the garment bag and shoes away from her. "I thought I asked you to bring these to me? How did you end up with Alexa instead?"

Drea let her brother take the items from her hands. "Like you didn't know that I would try to deliver them myself? You know me better than that. Now you'd better talk Alexa into coming to the party—or else. I will be very disappointed if you can't work your legendary charm on her." Drea grinned and waved at me and headed back towards the house.

"I thought we agreed that you and I would catch up with each other tomorrow, Drake."

"No, you told me to find you in the morning. I never agreed to anything. I decided that plan doesn't really work for me. Come to the party tonight." Drake's eyes drilled into mine as though he could glare me into accepting his invitation.

"I don't think it's a good idea. We barely know each other. You still have some explaining to do, and everyone is going to get the wrong idea about us. Look at your sister. She seems to think that I am your girlfriend. We've barely even spoken to each other! And how the heck does your sister know what size shoe I wear?"

Drake's eyes turn even darker in color, glinting with humor, as he shook his head at me. "No can do, babe. I don't care if anyone thinks you're my girlfriend because you're going to be. I told Drea your shoe size. I asked your dad in the car while you were zoned out. Take this stuff and go get ready. I'll be back for you in an hour. We can talk before the party starts."

"But—" I shook my head in denial, and Drake didn't even let me continue.

"Nope." He reached over and placed his index finger over my lips, instantly quieting my argument. "You can deny it all you want, but I know that you can feel the chemistry between us. When I saw you at the Sig Chi party with Jackson, I wanted you right away. I thought I couldn't have you, and it pissed me off. I was wrong. I've never been so happy to be wrong about something. 'Cause believe me when I say that I'm going to have you, and I'm not sure I'm going to want to let you go again."

I didn't know what to say. His confession shocked the hell out of me! I felt like he was steamrolling over me, and I really wanted to cave. His finger caressed my lips as he waited for my response. I'd felt this thing between us, but I just didn't know if I could trust him.

"I'll come to the party with you. We'll talk, but that's all that's going to happen tonight. Understand?"

"Okay, babe. I hear you. Keep in mind that it isn't tonight yet." He leaned towards me and his lips crushed against mine. His tongue licked the seam of my mouth, and he nibbled on my lower lip. My brain turned to mush, and my body started to tremble in response. My eyes drifted closed as I enjoyed our first kiss.

Drake groaned deep in his throat, and I could feel the vibrations through the kiss. He pecked the corner of my lips and pulled away from me. Handing me the bags, he nudged me through the door before I could react. My head was still spinning.

"One hour. Be ready for me," he said before turning around and striding away from me. Damn, I was going to be in so much trouble with this guy. *There is just no controlling my response to him,* I thought as I watched his ass until I couldn't see him anymore.

Shutting the door, I heard my dad clear his throat behind me. "Still nothing to say about Drake?" He smirked at me, and I blushed. He had definitely caught us kissing. Drat! "Sounds like you need to go get ready for a party, honey. Aren't you glad you decided to come with me this trip?"

I lightly punched him in the arm. "Geesh, Dad. You're such a smartass sometimes. The normal response would be for you to threaten Drake with bodily harm if he touches me again. Not to taunt me about kissing him and going to a party. And didn't you think it was odd that he asked you my shoe size? You just told him it without asking any questions?"

"It's about time I saw you interested in a boy again, Alexa. I know that everything that happened with Brad scared you off relationships, but you need to learn to let people into your life. Even boys. Go to this party with Drake and have some fun. I'm right here, so nothing bad will happen to you. You're safe. Live a little already!"

"All right, Daddy. I'll go to the party with Drake. But don't get your hopes up about relationships and stuff. I don't know what's going on with him, but Drake has a lot of explaining to do. Maybe we'll get a chance to talk tonight and work some things out. That doesn't make him my boyfriend though."

My dad laughed and shook his head at me. "I heard him plain as day, honey. If he has his way, he will absolutely be your boyfriend. Mark my words. Good thing I like him."

I headed upstairs and opened the bag. Inside was a stunning cocktail dress. The deep purple color was almost an exact match to the dress I'd worn last night. What were the odds that Drake's sister would pick out something in my favorite color? I held the dress up to my body as I looked in the mirror, stunned at the thought that he might have been specific with his sister in what he wanted me to wear tonight.

I hadn't brought many hair products or makeup with me. The downside of packing light and bringing my study materials, I guess. I wasn't sure that my usual brush of powder across my face and touch of chapstick would do the dress justice, but it wasn't like I had many options. Better to show the real me now so Drake knew what to expect going forward anyway. If he was expecting a frilly, girlie-girl, then he was going to be very surprised.

I pulled the shoes out of the box and gasped when I realized they matched the dress perfectly. They weren't the heels I had been expecting. They were beautiful ballet flats, a deep purple patent leather with a red sole that couldn't have been worn very much since they looked practically brand new except for a couple scratches on the bottom. They could only mean one thing. He had definitely told his sister what to find, and he'd based his instructions on what he had seen me wearing last night. This meant that he really had seen me and had been as drawn to me as I had been to him. It didn't make any sense. If he had noticed everything I'd worn, down to my preference for flats, then why hadn't he said anything to me?

Chapter 6

A N HOUR HAD never passed so quickly. Before I knew it, I could hear Drake's knock on the door downstairs. My dad made it to the door before I had even reached the top of the stairs. Curious to see what they would say to each other, I paused at the landing so I could eavesdrop.

"Hello, Mr. Hewitt. Is Alexa almost ready to go?" Drake asked as he stepped into the house.

"I'm not sure, son. She hasn't come down yet, but I expect she'll be ready soon," my dad responded.

"I hope so," Drake offered. "The party will start soon, but I wanted to show her some of the property before we joined everyone. I didn't think to ask earlier, but you're more than welcome to come up to the house for the party, too."

"Thanks, but I'm fine down here. Got some football to watch and snacks to eat. Not much for big parties anyway," I heard my dad say. "Besides, you'll be lucky to get Lex up to the party after your walk. She's hard to rile, but once you get her going, you'd better watch out."

"She has every right to be mad at me right now. I wasn't very nice to her when we met, and I know that I owe her an explanation. I promise—"

My dad put his hand up to stop Drake mid-sentence. "Make your explanations and promises to her first. If she accepts what you've got to say and wants to date you, just understand that you'll answer to me if you hurt her in any way. And that's a big if, boy. She deserves someone good in her life, and you'll be damn lucky if she gives you the chance to be that person."

On that note, I stepped out of the shadows and started down the stairs. I was happy that Drake had thought to include my dad in the invitation for the party, and I wasn't surprised that he didn't want to go. I was surprised to hear my dad open up about me though. He must have been more concerned about my lack of a dating life than I'd realized. The experience with Brad hadn't just affected me. It had hurt my dad, too.

Drake and my father heard me as I moved down the stairs and turned their heads toward me. My dad's face was filled with pride as he looked at me with such love. I had no doubt that he would always have my back, supporting me through anything that might come my way. I reached for him as soon as I got near and hugged him tight. "Love you, Daddy," I whispered into his ear.

I glanced towards Drake as my dad kissed my cheek, his arms tightening around me. He was staring at me, a look of hunger flashing across his face. As my dad let me go, Drake's expression cleared and he smiled at both of us.

"Alexa." He reached his hand out to me. "Ready? You look great."

"It's the outfit that's great. Thanks for thinking of me."

"No, it's definitely you. Trust me on that at least." He tugged me closer to him. "We've got some time before the party kicks off, and I'd like to show you around a bit. You up for a walk?"

"As long as talking is included with the walking, I'm fine with that. Bye, Dad." I let Drake lead me out the door.

"Night, Alexa. I'll be here if you need anything. Don't forget, this might not be my roof, but I still expect you back at a decent hour. We have the flight back tomorrow, and you need your wits about you if you're going to take the controls again."

"Geesh, Dad. I know—" I started to respond. Drake's hand tightened around mine, and he shook his head.

"No, Alexa. Your dad is only looking out for you. I understand where he's coming from. I need to earn his trust as much as I do yours." He looked my dad straight in the eyes with a determined look.

"I swear she'll come to no harm with me. Not now, not ever. I'll have her back to you with plenty of time for a good night's sleep tonight."

"Glad to know you hear what I'm saying, Drake." My dad stretched his hand out and offered it to Drake. As they shook hands, I could feel Drake relax beside me, as though a weight had been lifted off his shoulders.

Drake grabbed my hand again after their handshake ended. "C'mon, Alexa. We'd better head out so we have enough time to talk before my mom sends out a search party."

We wandered past the stables and towards a gazebo surrounded by flowers. Drake explained that his mom loved gardening as much as his sister loved horses. By all appearances, what his dad must love is to indulge both his wife and daughter. Drake settled me onto a bench in the gazebo. With the garden around us and strings of lights twinkling above, the setting was terribly romantic. He sat down next to me and turned so he could look me in the eyes.

"I know I've been a bit of a jerk to you, Alexa. I've already apologized, but I haven't had a chance to explain." He leaned in towards me and wrapped his hands around mine.

"A bit? I think I have whiplash from your mood shifts. You seemed interested in the store this morning until I told you we'd met at the party. Then you flirted hard before you recognized me on the plane after that. What could I have possibly done to deserve that treatment?"

He lifted my hands to his lips and kissed them. I could feel his breath on them as he sighed. "Nothing. You didn't do anything, and I shouldn't have taken my frustration out on you. I've noticed you around campus the last couple weeks. Couldn't get you out of my head. There was just something about you that pulled me in. You stood out among all the other girls at school. It wasn't just that you're hot because there are plenty of hot girls at school. I hadn't even talked to you, and I was already comparing chicks to you when they flirted with me. Couldn't work up any interest for anyone else, so I decided to talk to you the next time I saw you. Ended up that it was at the party last night instead of on campus at lunch or in the quad. And then I saw Jackson with you, and I was pissed that he got to you first."

I shook my head in confusion. It seemed like he and Jackson

were friendly last night. This didn't make any sense to me. "Why would it matter that I know Jackson? I don't understand."

"It's like this. There's a guy code that I follow. Bros before hos—not that I am saying you are a ho or anything like that. I like Jackson. He seems like a cool guy from the time we've hung out together. I thought you were with him at the party. That he'd gotten to you before me, and if he had then I would have to respect that."

"You thought that Jackson and I were a couple?"

Drake shook his head at me and glared. "Let me finish, babe. I need to get this out and on the table. For the first time ever, I didn't want to follow the rule. I wanted you with me and not him. I had to watch you walk away with him, up the stairs to his room. I spent the rest of the night pissed the fuck off, imagining what you guys were doing in his room. I left the party and stayed away so that I wouldn't knock his door down to get to you."

His hands had clenched around mine, squeezing hard. He looked so angry with his eyes blazing into mine.

"Never been knocked off my feet like that before. I hadn't planned to come home this weekend because I had too much going on at school. Seeing you at the party fucked with my head so much that I needed to get away so I had my dad book the charter out here. Wanted some distance to get my head on straight before I saw Jackson again at the frat house. Wasn't sure I could see him without smashing my fist into his face."

He chuckled darkly and looked at the ground as he admitted the anger he felt. "Then I bumped into you at the store this morning. You looked so different, but I still felt the chemistry. When I realized it was you again, I felt like karma really was a bitch. Grabbed my mom's card and headed back to my apartment to pack my stuff up. Only there you were again when I got on the plane. I was trying to run from you, and I just couldn't get the fuck away."

He looked back up at me, and his hands gentled on mine. He lips turned up in a grin. "Hearing you say that you've known his mom as long as you've known him was probably the best news I've heard in a long time. I realized that what I'd seen between you wasn't what I'd thought it was. Meant that you were free for me to pursue."

He looked at me expectantly after his announcement. "Oh, is it my turn to speak now?" I asked with sarcasm, masking the whirl of thoughts flying through my mind.

His eyes flared with heat at my show of irritation. "Yeah, I'm done for now. Go ahead, babe."

"Not so sure I like you calling me babe, babe."

Drake leaned closer to me, our noses brushing against each other. His lips were as close to mine as they could be without us kissing. "Oh, you're going to like me calling you babe. Trust me on that."

I shook my head, hoping to clear my thoughts as my skin broke out in goose bumps. "You did get it wrong. Jackson is like a big brother to me. His sister is my best friend, and we've known each other since kindergarten."

"Glad to hear confirmation that there isn't anything going on between you two. Not sure I'd be able to back off at this point anyway. You'd be worth the risk," Drake replied. "Doesn't explain why Jackson didn't introduce us or why he bailed on the party to hang out with you in his room though."

His eyes had hardened again. Clearly the thought of me spending time in Jackson's room wasn't a pleasant thought for Drake. "Jackson's a little protective of me with guys. I'm not sure if that's why he didn't introduce us. You'd have to ask him. And he knew that the party wasn't really my scene so he helped me make my escape for a little while. We hung out and watched a movie in his room so that I didn't bail so early that Aubrey would be pissed at me."

"Is that a normal thing for you two, hanging out in his room and watching movies?" Drake didn't look very happy with my explanation.

"Every day normal? No. Happens from time to time? Yes." I knew my tone was getting snippy, but I didn't feel like he had any right to question my perfectly innocent friendship with Jackson.

"Just want to make sure I understand the situation right. Could have sworn that I saw something between the two of you."

"I don't know what you think you saw, but I can tell you that you were wrong if it was anything other than close friendship. Jackson's protective of me because he feels responsible after the way my last relationship ended. Maybe that's what you saw."

Drake's head snapped up when I mentioned the end of my relationship with Brad. "Is there a reason he should feel responsible for you ending things with your boyfriend?"

"No! That's not what I said at all. Things got messy, and Jackson had to step into the middle of it for me. End of story." There's no way I was going to share everything with Drake now. If he managed to dig himself out of the hole he'd put himself in and things progressed between us, then I'd think about sharing more. Maybe.

"I'll accept that. For now. But I don't want any secrets between us. You got a problem or a question, I want you to come to me. I get that Jackson's been there for you in the past, but I'm gonna be the one there for you in the future."

I held my hand up in protest. "Whoa. Slow down there, buddy."

He reached up and tweaked my nose. "I get it. I'm jumping ahead of myself. No pressure. We've got plenty of time because I'm not going anywhere. Now that we've got all that past us, we'd better hit my mom's party. I'm sure she's wondering where we're at by now."

Drake's parents seemed nice and were happy to have me join them. Drea was serious about introducing me to everyone and stole me away from Drake the minute we joined the party. She dragged me around the room, flitting from group to group, and refused to listen when I told her I wasn't Drake's girlfriend. Drake certainly didn't help at all as he followed after us laughing.

He kept his word and didn't even give me so much as a peck on the cheek when he walked me back to the pool house at the end of the night. I tried to tell myself this was a good thing as I needed the time to wrap my head around our conversation from earlier. Yet I couldn't stop myself from wishing that he'd given me a goodnight kiss. I already craved the feel of his lips on mine.

I tossed and turned through the night, torn by my fears of jumping into a relationship with Drake and my desires. I dreamed of us together, bodies entwined. The feel of his hard body crushed against me, his lips devouring mine. The whisper of his strong fingers gliding down my body, teasing me to the point of frenzy. My legs writhing together as my body clenched in anticipation. I awoke, drenched in sweat, my heart beating thunderously. I gasped for breath when my body pulsed as a climax rolled over me.

Holy crap! Even in my dreams, the attraction between us was insanely hot! I actually came because of a dream of Drake. Just a dream. I didn't know if I wanted to find him right this minute so I could jump his bones or stay as far away from him as I possibly could. After everything that had happened with Brad, I hadn't so much as noticed another guy in a sexual way. Drake was another story altogether. I couldn't stop myself from thinking about him. Great timing for my hormones to jump back to life.

Luckily, the morning flew by. I'd jumped in the shower and had a quick breakfast with my dad before we were to head to the airport. Drake had stopped by while I was in the shower to see if I wanted to eat with him. Dad had already been working on a batch of pancakes with yummy maple syrup and fresh strawberries. It was my favorite breakfast, and Dad wanted to surprise me. Drake couldn't join us since his parents had expected him to share breakfast with them, so I'd had a reprieve from seeing him for a little bit.

When we met outside at the car, Drake wrapped me into a deep hug that seemed to last forever. He huffed as he let me go. "Missed you this morning, babe."

I pushed myself away from him. "Drake, please stop."

He raised a brow at me as I stepped away. "Not gonna happen. My dad raised me to go after what I want, and I want you. Thought I'd made that clear last night."

I shook my head at him in frustration. "Yes, you made your intentions crystal clear. But I still need time to decide what I want to do about them."

"Just don't push me away. I can handle the wait, but I want you to give me a chance. Spend time with me. Let us get to know each other better, babe. You know you want to say yes."

"Fine! We can see each other when we get back on campus and see what happens. Okay?" I huffed in exasperation.

Drake's eyes beamed at me as he grinned. "Better than okay. Give me your cell. I need to make sure you can reach me."

I handed him my phone without really thinking about it. Before I knew it, his cell was ringing in his front pocket. My eyes followed his hand as he reached inside to pull his cell out. The phone snagged on his shirt and lifted it up to reveal his six-pack abs. He pulled the phone away and chuckled when he realized I was staring.

"Hey! What are you doing?" I asked.

"Doesn't do me much good if you have my phone number but I don't have yours. I don't know that I can trust you to call me yet." Drake handed my phone back to me. I glanced at the screen and saw that he'd added himself to my contacts as 'Drake aka My Boyfriend.'

I couldn't help the giggle that escaped my lips before I changed the contact information to just his name. "Really? So you're my boyfriend now? After one sorta date at your parents' house?"

Drake shrugged his shoulders. "I'll take whatever edge I can get. Thought that subliminal messaging just might work on you."

"Subliminal messaging, huh?"

"A guy's gotta do what a guy's gotta do. You're not exactly making this easy on me."

"I only met you two nights ago and we've already kissed, been on a date, and met each other's parents. That doesn't exactly scream 'hard to get' to me."

Drake reached out and stroked my cheek. "True, but I've wanted you since I saw you weeks ago. Most other girls would've been in and out of my bed by now."

I snapped my head away from him. "Geesh, Drake. Talking about other girls isn't going to help you with me."

"It's not like I'm sharing details here. Just pointing out that you should never think of yourself as an easy conquest. I don't think of you that way at all. Now, are you and your dad ready to head back to campus?"

Arms crossed, I glared at Drake. I was a little irritated with him for putting the thought of him with other girls into my head. "Yes, we can leave whenever you want to go."

"Alexa, stop. I didn't say that to make you angry with me. We have lots to learn about each other, and we both have pasts. But that's all it is—the past. I'm not interested in having anyone else in my bed or in my life but you. I'm not the kind of guy who will blow smoke up your ass. You can trust me to tell you like it is, whether you want to hear something or not."

I shook my head in response. "I don't know you well enough to throw around the word trust about anything."

"But you will, babe. You'll know me better than anyone else.

And I'm gonna know you, inside and out. In every way possible."

I could feel the heat rising as I blushed in response to the images his words evoked of our bodies entwined. "Down, boy. I thought you said you were okay with the wait."

"I did, but I never said that I'd pussyfoot around with you. That's not my style. But I hear what you're saying. Let me know if I'm pushing too hard. Yeah?"

"Consider yourself warned that you're pushing then," I responded.

Drake raised his hands up in the air. "Gotcha. Backing off here."

The trip back to campus was uneventful. We rode to the airport in the same limousine, with Drake and my dad talking about sports again. Male bonding time, I guessed. At least it gave me time to rest before the flight since I was tired from my restless night. I curled up on the seat and leaned my head back so I could take a little nap. When we got to the airport, I awoke, disoriented, with my head on Drake's shoulder and his arm wrapped around my shoulders. My dad sat across from us and smiled indulgently at me as I stretched.

"You sure you're alert enough to co-pilot? You seem awfully tired, Alexa," he asked.

"Yeah, Dad. I'm fine. I had a little trouble settling down to sleep last night. That catnap helped a lot though," I answered.

"Alexa's welcome to rest with me in the cabin if she wants," Drake offered.

I was tempted to skip out on co-piloting, but I could easily imagine the temptation Drake would provide for me instead of resting while we were alone. "No, thanks. I need more hours logged in the Lear, Drake."

I jumped out of the car as soon as it rolled to a stop. I needed a moment away from Drake so I could pull myself together. My defenses were down, and I wasn't ready to move forward so quickly with him.

"Alexa, you okay?" I heard Drake ask from behind me as his hand skated up my spine.

I turned and smiled at Drake. "Yup, everything's okay. I'm just excited to get back in the cockpit."

Drake chuckled and said huskily, "I'd love to hear you say cock in a totally different setting, babe."

I punched him on the shoulder and shushed him. "Drake, my dad is right over there!"

He held up his hands in mock surrender. "Got it, babe. I'll save it for later when we're alone. Go do what you need to do to get ready for the flight. I'll see you when we land."

Chapter 7

BY THE TIME we got back to town, Drake had to run so he'd make it to his team meeting on time. He wanted to drop me at my dorm first, but my car was already at the airport. I raced to the dorm to meet Aubrey. I'd sent her a text when we landed to make sure she was there. Luckily, Faith and Natalie were gone for the day, so we'd have some privacy. I needed her advice about Drake. She had a lot more experience than I did with boys and relationships.

Aubrey was waiting for me with the makings for sundaes set out. She had all my favorites—vanilla ice cream, caramel sauce, whipped cream, and cherries. "Comfort food! It sounded like something was up in your text. Sounded like a sundae occasion to me!"

"Damn! That's why I love you, girl. Just what I needed." I gave Aubrey a hug and started to pile ice cream into a bowl. I was generous with the toppings I added before we settled onto the couch.

"What's up? Did something happen with your dad on the trip?" Aubrey asked.

"You won't believe who our passenger was. Drake fucking Bennett," I answered.

Aubrey's jaw practically hit the floor. "Shut the front door! Seriously? Is that what has your undies in a bunch?"

I shook my head. "Nope. Flying with Drake as a passenger wasn't that big of a deal. Finding out that he's interested in me threw me for a curve. Going to his mom's birthday party was a little different. Kissing him and having him pretty much telling me that I am going to be his girlfriend? Yeah, that's enough to make me a little crazy."

Aubrey squealed. "Yikes! Sounds like you were wrong. Third time was the charm with him. What did he say? Did he kiss you or did you kiss him? C'mon, dish already!"

I recapped the trip for her, sparing very few details. By the time I was done, she was on the edge of her seat, her sundae sitting forgotten on the table. Apparently, the idea of me having a love life that featured Drake Bennett was more interesting than ice cream. Go figure.

"So when are you going to see him again?" she asked.

I shrugged my shoulders. "I'm not sure. He had to get back to campus for some rugby thing. We swapped phone numbers. I'm not sure when he'll call."

Aubrey wagged her finger at me. "Uhm, no! You don't have to wait for him to call. Take the initiative and make the next move. He made it clear that he's interested. There's a ton of girls on campus who would die for a chance like this. Go for it!"

I held my hand up to stop her rant. "No way! That's not gonna happen. I'm not even sure that I want to date Drake in the first place. He seems like a player to me. The last thing I need is another cheating boyfriend."

Aubrey just laughed at me. "Lex, no! You can't think that way. You have to start dating sometime, and I will kill you if you pass up this opportunity. You haven't noticed another guy in two years, but you perked right up when you mentioned Drake yesterday morning. You're interested in him, aren't you?"

I shoved a big spoonful of ice cream into my mouth and pointed at my face to indicate that I couldn't talk. Aubrey leveled a stare at me until I finally broke. "Okay, okay. I admit that he's hot, but does that really mean I should date him? Maybe now that my hormones are awake, I'll start noticing other guys too."

"I know you're scared to trust someone again. Dating a new guy is scary no matter what. After Brad, it has to be even more frightening for you. But you aren't going to go out and find someone you are barely attracted to just so you can try to protect yourself. That's just crazy." Aubrey looked disappointed in me. "Besides, you already told Drake you would give him a chance. You just told me so yourself. Are you going to go back on your word? Because I don't think he's the type of guy who will let you get away with that."

My cell phone chimed with a text message

.

Drake: Free tonite?

Aubrey snatched the phone from my hand to read the message and typed out a response before I could react.

Alexa: Yes!
Drake: Dinner?
Alexa: Where?
Drake: You pick. Pick you up at 8.
Alexa: K

I chased Aubrey around the room as she replied to each of Drake's messages. "Woo-hoo! You have a dinner date with Drake tonight at eight. No backing out now!"

Aubrey handed my phone to me, and I read through the conversation. "Aubrey! I told you that I wasn't sure I wanted to date Drake. Whose side are you on anyway?"

"Yours. I am always on your side. No matter what. That's why I'm telling you to go on this date. Drake's hot and seriously interested in you. If he ends up being a total ass, you'll find out before you get in too deep with him. I'll just ask Jackson for all the dirt on Drake. I'll have all the details for you when you get home tonight. Promise." She swept her finger across her heart in a cross motion.

There was a knock on our door promptly at eight. Faith and Natalie were both hanging out in the common area so they could get a glimpse of Drake before we left for dinner. Aubrey had told them about the date and threatened them with bodily harm if they flirted too much with him when he picked me up. Her warning didn't stop either of the girls from primping before he showed though.

Aubrey waved them away and answered the door. "Hey, Drake. Not sure if you remember me. Aubrey Silver, Jackson's sister and Alexa's best friend."

Drake nodded his head. "Yeah, I've seen you around with Jackson. Nice to see you."

Aubrey waved Drake into the room. "These are our suite mates, Faith and Natalie."

Drake lifted his chin in greeting at the girls on the couch, his eyes locked on me. They giggled and whispered to each other.

Drake came over to me and pulled my body towards his. "Babe, you look fantastic! I'm starved. Ready to go?" he whispered into my ear with his husky voice.

I shivered in response and just nodded my head. I felt his lips graze my ear as he pulled away to look at me.

"You okay?"

"Yes, I'm fine. Just really hungry," I answered.

"Let's get you fed. Can't have you starving on my watch." We waved goodbye to my roommates, and Drake took possession of my hand as we walked out of the dorm. He laced his fingers through mine and held on tight, like he thought I was going to pull away.

He led me to a Dodge Viper parked illegally at the curb in front of the dorm and opened the passenger door. Once I was settled into my seat with the door closed, he went to his side of the car and climbed into the driver's seat. The car smelled like Drake, I inhaled deeply and closed my eyes.

Drake looked over at me as he started the engine. "You doing breathing exercises over there?"

My eyes snapped open, and I blushed. I was embarrassed to have been caught sniffing his car, but I wasn't about to admit to it. "Nope, just trying to catch my breath."

"I take your breath away, huh?" Drake flashed me a sexy smirk in response.

He really could be a cocky bastard. "Not what I said. It's been a busy day, and I'm starving. I'm happy to have a moment to relax and think about food."

Drake chuckled in response. "Sure, that's what you were doing. Where am I taking you to satisfy that hunger of yours?"

"Do you like Italian?" I asked. "Ciao Bella is probably my favorite restaurant in town."

Drake picked up my hand and placed a light kiss into my palm. He put my hand on his thigh and squeezed before he pulled the car away from the curb. "Sounds good to me. I like the idea of feeding you your favorite foods."

I could feel the heat from his body through his jeans. His muscles clenched as he pressed the gas, and it took all my willpower not to squeeze his thigh. My hand still tingled where he'd kissed it, and my heart was racing. "It's downtown, across the street from the library."

I sat in silence, darting occasional glances his way as we drove to the restaurant. It was only a few minutes from campus and served fantastic food. I'd been going there since I was little, so it seemed like a safe place for our first date. When we pulled up in front, Drake opted to use the valet service. He hopped out of the car and waved the attendant away from my side of the car to help me out himself.

I smiled up at him, happy that he had opened the door for me. "Good manners. Your mom would be proud."

"I'm sure she would, but it doesn't have anything to do with the manners my mom taught me. Don't need to give another guy an excuse to get up close and personal to you." Drake tugged me into his side as we walked into the restaurant.

The hostess who greeted us wasn't one I recognized from my previous visits. She was young, probably still in high school, and she stared at Drake as he asked for a table for two with some privacy. He smiled at her while making his request, and she giggled in response without looking my way even once.

"Right this way," she sighed as she sashayed her way to our table, swaying her hips while she walked in front of us. I glanced over at Drake, expecting his eyes to be glued to her ass. I was surprised to find him staring at me instead, a twinkle in his eye. He rolled his eyes at me and shook his head as he glanced at the hostess. I felt so much better knowing that he found her actions amusing instead of attractive.

She gave Drake exactly what he'd asked for—a booth in the corner, away from the other diners. As she placed the menus on the table, Drake ushered me into the booth and squeezed in next to me. The hostess huffed a little as she finally noticed me. She gave Drake a secret little smile before walking away.

"That happen often?" I asked.

"What?" Drake acted like he had no idea what I was talking about as he glanced at the menu. "Any recommendations for what's good here?"

I shook my head and let him change the subject. It wasn't like he had control over how other people acted around him, and he hadn't done anything to make the girl think he was interested the way other guys might have done. "Yes, anything with pasta."

Drake glanced down at the menu and scanned the contents. "Babe, everything has pasta."

"Exactly. I've never eaten here and not liked the food. You can order whatever you like. Trust me. It will be delicious," I quipped back as the waiter approached our table.

"Alexa, welcome back!" Tony greeted me. "I didn't know you were coming in for dinner tonight. Is your dad joining you?" Tony started working at Ciao Bella about a year ago. It seemed like he was always assigned to my section whenever I came in.

"Hi, Tony. No, Dad isn't having dinner with us tonight," I replied.

Drake draped his arm across my shoulders as we spoke. Tony glanced his way and his expression seemed to fall as he realized that I was on a date. "Ahhh, date night, huh?" he asked.

"Yeah, man," Drake practically growled in response. "Could you bring us a bottle of Chianti to start?"

"I'm sorry, sir. I can't serve Alexa alcohol since she isn't twenty-one. May I see your ID? I can bring you some wine if you'd like. Alexa, how about an iced tea?" Tony offered.

Drake turned to me. "You're not twenty-one yet?"

"Nope. I'm only twenty. I have several months to go 'til my birthday. Sorry," I apologized.

"No apology needed. Guess I figured you for older with the whole pilot thing," Drake said. He glanced up at Tony. "How about two iced teas then?"

Tony nodded and left to get our drinks.

"How do you know the waiter?" Drake asked.

"Just from the restaurant. My dad and I come here a couple times a month," I answered. "I know a lot of people around here. The benefits of being a townie."

Drake tightened his hold on me. "He better keep his eyes off you before I feel the need to do something about it."

"Seriously? He didn't even do anything. At least he spoke to you, unlike the hostess, who acted like I didn't exist," I scoffed.

"I finally have you to myself. Not real excited that our waiter has a crush on you, but I'll handle it," Drake whispered into my ear. Shivers raced up my spine as he nuzzled my neck.

"Your drinks," Tony said as he placed our iced teas in front of us. "The usual tonight, Alexa?"

"Yes, please. Drake? Have you decided what you'd like to try?" I turned my head to look at Drake as I asked him what he wanted. He was glaring at the waiter with icy eyes. I nudged him in the side to draw his attention, and his face softened as he looked at me.

"The manicotti for me," he ordered and I giggled. "Why is that funny? I thought you said anything with pasta is good here. Should I order something else?"

I giggled harder as Tony explained. "That's Alexa's favorite dish here. She orders it every time she comes in."

"Great minds think alike. If you love it that much, then I'm looking forward to trying it tonight." Drake smirked at me.

Drake and I talked about school until the food came. We were juniors this year but didn't have any classes together. It was odd since we were both Business majors and we went to a small school. Turned out that Drake was further along in his studies than I was, even after the transfer over to Blythe. I hadn't declared my major until this year, so I was a little behind on my required classes for graduation.

"Another reason to date me. I can tutor you whenever you need it," Drake offered before finishing his last bite. "Not like you should need more reasons anyway."

I pushed my plate away. Even though I was hungry, I couldn't finish it with all the butterflies flitting around inside my stomach. "I don't need tutoring. Just more time in the day. But thanks for the offer."

Tony appeared at the table, hovering over us attentively. I could tell he was still getting on Drake's nerves.

"Can you box this up for me to go?" I asked Tony. "We need to head out."

"Sure. I'll be right back with your doggy bag and the check," Tony replied.

"We have plans I don't know about?" Drake teased.

"No, I just figured we could use a change of scenery," I answered. "Wanna grab some gelato next door?"

Drake pulled his wallet from his back pocket. "I could eat gelato. You want some, then let's do that."

He paid the bill and left Tony a nice tip, surprising me since there was tension between the two all night.

He noticed me looking at the credit card slip as he signed it. "I can afford to be generous. I get to leave with you, and he gets to go home with his tip money. No contest, babe."

I scooted out of the booth and stepped to the side so Drake could get out also. He grabbed my hand as we walked out, flashing a grin at Tony on the way. Wanting to make him realize how ridiculous he was being, I smirked at the hostess as she ogled Drake when we went past her.

"Not very good with sharing. Get used to it," Drake responded to my action as he snuggled me into his side. It was a little cool outside, and the heat from his body warmed me. "You cold?"

"I'm surprised it cooled down this much tonight. Wasn't expecting the change in weather yet," I answered. Here I was, on a date with a hot guy, and I was talking about the weather. I really had been out of the dating scene too long.

"Too cold for gelato?" he asked.

"No way! It's never too cold for ice cream of any kind. It's kind of an addiction of mine." I smiled shyly up at him.

Drake opened the door of the gelato shop and ushered me through. "An addiction, huh? I'll have to keep that in mind in case I ever need to bribe you in the future. I'm sure that information will be put to good use when I do something stupid."

"I'll have to be careful about sharing all my secrets if you're keeping track of them." I punched him in the shoulder.

"Be careful all you want, Alexa. I'm going to learn your secrets one way or another. Now give me another one. What's your favorite flavor?"

I ordered a rich vanilla swirled with caramel. Drake got the chocolate. We sat at a table near the window and watched people walk by as we ate our gelato. My eyes closed as I savored the last bite of mine, a small moan escaping. I heard Drake's spoon clatter on the table and opened my eyes to find him staring at me with a hungry expression on his face. He'd barely touched his double scoop.

"Is it too chocolaty for your tastes?" I asked.

"No. The gelato is fine. It's just not what I'm hungry for right now." Drake licked his lips and flashed a sexy grin my way.

"I'm not touching that comment with a ten-foot pole!" I joked.

"How about a ten-inch pole?" Drake glanced down at his lap and wagged his eyebrows.

I laughed so hard in response that I snorted. I hadn't laughed like this with a guy ever. Sure, I joked around with Jackson, but he didn't really count since he was like a brother to me. "Yeah, yeah. I walked right into that one, didn't I?"

Drake just smiled and nodded. He spooned up a scoop of his gelato and held it to my lips. "Here, why don't you have a taste of mine?"

I opened my mouth, and Drake slid the spoon inside. I'd had the chocolate here before, but I'd swear that it didn't taste as good then as it did now as I licked it from Drake's spoon. He gently pulled the spoon past my lips and glanced down at it. "Damn. I'm jealous of a frickin' utensil. You're killing me here."

He popped the spoon into his mouth and sucked the remaining gelato from it. His eyes were glued to my mouth, and I gasped as I watched him. "Drake," I sighed out his name.

Drake grabbed the containers off the table and pulled me to my feet. He practically dragged me from the shop, tossing everything in the trash on our way out the door. He didn't say a word or look my way as we waited while the valet brought the car around. He just kept my hand gripped tightly in his as he breathed deeply next to me. When the valet pulled up, Drake yanked the passenger car door open and helped me into the car. After he climbed in, he clenched the steering wheel before starting the car.

The tension in the car was overwhelming. "Drake," I said softly, looking for reassurance that I hadn't done anything wrong.

"Shhh, Alexa. Just needed to get out of there before I did something we both regretted. The sight of your lips wrapped around that spoon. Your eyes on me as I savored the taste of you mixed with chocolate. Then that damn sigh. I swear to you that you will make that same fucking sound again, but next time it'll be in my ear with my cock deep inside your pussy," Drake rasped.

His words stunned me. My heart sped up as he spoke, and I broke out in a sweat. My pussy clenched and dripped in reaction. I could practically see sexual sparks flying between us as I turned to look at him.

"Drake," I repeated.

"No, Alexa. You say one more word and I won't be liable for what I do next. I'm hanging by a thread here, babe. Unless you want me to find the nearest hotel with an empty bed in it, stop saying my name like that."

I stared at him as he drove back to campus. His chiseled jaw was clenched. There was no sign of the dimple that usually flashed when he laughed. No smiling twinkle in his eye. No softness in his gaze as he sent a heated look my way. It felt like time had become suspended, but before I knew it we were parked in front of my dorm again.

Drake cut off the engine and turned his body towards me. He unclipped his seatbelt and pocketed his keys, but he didn't move to exit the car. His eyes had darkened to the color of melted chocolate, and a flush spread across his cheekbones. I stayed silent, trying not to push him over the edge.

"I want you more than I've ever wanted anyone before, but I know you aren't ready to hop in between the sheets with me yet. You're different, special. Gotta make sure I treat you right." Drake reached across and stroked his thumb over my cheek as he held my chin in his hand. "Now isn't the time for this. I know that in my head, but fuck if my body will listen to reason."

A giggle bubbled up in my throat. I had a horrible tendency to laugh at the most inopportune times, usually out of nervousness. Drake's lips tilted into a sexy grin in response.

"Something funny about that to you? 'Cause my dick sure isn't laughing right now."

My giggles turned into full-out laughter, so hard that tears rolled down my cheeks. The tension broke as Drake joined in, chuckling in response to my hilarity. As we settled down, I figured it was safe for me to talk again.

"Really? Does your dick laugh often, Drake?" I asked.

He just shook his head in response. "No, babe. It doesn't. What time's your first class tomorrow?"

"Pretty early. I have Macroeconomics at eight a.m." I answered.

"You gonna walk to class?" Drake asked.

I nodded my head. "Yeah, I always walk to my classes."

Drake leaned closer to me. "I'll meet you here before and walk you over then."

"You gonna carry my books, too?" I quipped back.

He tilted his head down until his lips rested directly in front of mine, a whisper of space between us. "Sure, why the hell not. Never carried a girl's books before. It'll be a first for me."

I licked my lips, and Drake's tongue darted out and flicked against mine. As my lips closed, Drake's mouth gently caressed mine. His breath was warm against my skin as he kept the kiss light. He pulled away, and I licked my lips again, tasting the chocolate flavor from his gelato.

Drake groaned and turned away from me. He climbed out of the car and opened my door. I stepped out and right into his space. Drake kept me trapped by the car for a moment as he looked down at me. I was convinced he was going to kiss me again, but he took a step backwards to let me pass by. "Go on up, and I'll see you in the morning."

"'Kay," I answered as I walked past. I felt a light slap on my ass and swiveled my head to look at Drake. "Hey!" I yelped.

Drake smirked in response and nodded his head towards the dorm. I could feel his eyes on me as I walked into the dorm. As the door closed behind me, I looked back and saw Drake watching me from the car, making sure I made it inside okay. His concern for my safety warmed me inside. I felt like he wanted more from me than just sex, even though we hadn't known each other long. If he was playing with me, he was doing a good job of sucking me into his trap. I wasn't sure how long I'd be able to keep myself out of his bed when I melted any time he was near.

Chapter 8

I FOUND DRAKE waiting for me outside the dorm the next morning when I left for class. He was leaning against the wall next to the doorway, legs crossed at the ankle while he played with his phone. I paused a moment so I could drink him in before he noticed me. His hair was darker than usual, still a little damp from the shower. His athletic body was totally relaxed, a stark contrast to the tension that seemed to permeate the air whenever we were together.

As my gaze drifted across his chest and trailed back up to his face, I realized he had caught me staring. "See something you like?" he teased.

"Not much I see that I don't like," I retorted. "Arrogant boy."

"How am I arrogant if it's true?" He picked his backpack up from the ground next to him and straightened. As he walked towards me, I felt trapped in his dark gaze. "You haven't got much room to talk, Alexa. You've gotta know that guys like what they see when they look at you. You might not play it up all the time, but you're fucking hot."

"If that's true, then you better carry my stuff so everyone knows we're together, huh?" I held out my bag, not expecting him to take it from me.

Drake snatched the bag from my fingertips and hefted it onto his shoulder. "I'll make it damn clear you're with me, babe. Don't doubt it for a second. Now gimme a kiss to make looking pussy-whipped worth it."

I snorted at his grumbling tone and gave him a quick peck on the cheek. "There. That's all you've earned today, errand boy."

Drake's free hand snaked out and wrapped around the back of my head, holding me in place. "Errand boy? I'm going for love slave here! I know you can do better than that. Guess I'll just have to steal my own damn kiss."

He pressed his lips against mine. I could feel their warmth all the way down to my toes as they curled in response. I parted my lips, and Drake's tongue swept into my mouth and rubbed against mine. My fingers trailed over his back as he deepened the kiss. I felt a sharp tug on my hair as he groaned and pulled away from me.

"Much better. That might last me until later today."

In a daze, I walked hand in hand with Drake across campus toward the academic buildings. People threw greetings our way, and we got a lot of surprised glances aimed at us. For someone new to campus, he sure seemed to know a lot of people already. And many of them were women who glared at me when they saw his hold on my hand and my bag on his shoulder. He just nodded in response to the guys and basically ignored the girls who tried to get his attention.

I gestured at the building we were walking toward. "How did you know where my class was?"

"I guessed it would be here and asked one of the guys at the house last night just to be sure. He's an Econ major, so I figured he'd know."

"Really? Didn't he find it weird that you needed to know?"

Drake chuckled deep in his throat. "Nah. He assumed it was about a girl. Why else would I give a fuck where I was going this early in the morning since my first class isn't 'til ten?"

"You woke up early just to walk me to class?"

He shrugged his shoulders. "Wanted to see you today and wasn't sure how our schedules would mesh. This way, I'll get some time with you and a workout in before class."

"Thank you, Drake. I'm surprised that you were willing to wake up so early for me, but it means a lot that you're making an effort to spend some time with me."

"Got a feeling you're going to be worth any effort I make."

I smiled and felt my walls coming down a little bit further. "Want to meet me for lunch today? I usually eat at the café on this side of campus instead of heading back to the cafeteria."

"I know, babe. I've seen you heading in as I've been on my way out. Already decided to crash your lunch. Now I don't have to since you invited me."

I just shook my head as he opened the door for me and ushered me inside. "Meet me there at noon?"

"Yeah, that works for me." He handed my bag to me and pushed a strand of hair behind my ear. "I have a feeling my day is going to creep by today, waiting for noon."

I watched him walk away, my enjoyment of the view interrupted by whispers and giggles behind me. I turned to find several girls staring at me. One of them looked familiar, and I realized she was the one who had been arguing with Drake when I saw him at the frat party. If looks could kill, I would definitely be six feet under. I walked past them as they stopped talking. It was pretty clear that Drake and I were the topic of conversation. I needed to remember to ask him what the hell was up with this girl. If she was an ex, then he needed to deal with it fast before I had to do something. If Aubrey caught wind of a bunch of sorority chicks giving me a hard time, all hell was going to break loose. My bestie always had my back, but her temper could get us into trouble.

My classes were pretty uneventful. I'd picked business as my major so I would be prepared to help my dad with the business side of things. I loved flying and was excited by the idea of being able to do it full time when I graduated in a couple years. Dad was adamant that I had to get a college education, but I'd be happy without one if it meant I could be in the cockpit now. He wanted me to be prepared in case I wanted to fly for one of the big airlines since they wouldn't hire me without the degree.

As I headed to the café for lunch, I could see Drake in the distance waiting for me. He was surrounded by a group of girls, including the blonde with the killer look earlier. Just what I needed. I slowed my pace down in the hope that their conversation would break up before I made it there. Walking slower than a snail, I felt a pair of hands grab me from behind and squealed out in surprise.

"Caught ya!" I heard Jackson say. "Whatcha doing, Lex?"

"Jackson, you scared the crap out of me!"

He turned me around and glanced at my butt. "Nope, don't see any crap there. You must be okay."

"Geesh, Jackson. You know what I meant. You can't sneak up on me like that."

He tweaked my nose and grinned down at me. "Gotta keep you on your toes, or I'll be falling down on the job. On your way to lunch?"

"Yeah," I sighed and glanced back over at Drake to find him staring at Jackson and me.

"Great! I'm starving. Let's grab some grub." He nudged me so I'd start walking again.

"I'm meeting Drake for lunch." I nodded my head in Drake's direction and noticed that he had broken away from the pack of girls and was heading our way fast.

"Drake?" Jackson asked, sounding surprised. "How did you meet him?"

"He chartered a flight with Dad this weekend and I went along to co-pilot."

"I'd heard around the frat house that he had something come up for his mom's birthday. Didn't even cross my mind when Aubrey mentioned you were flying with your dad that it would be for Drake." Jackson put a hand out to stop me so we could talk before Drake made it to us. "So you met him this weekend and you guys are meeting for lunch today?"

"Is that a problem?"

Jackson looked down at the ground and shook his head. "Not a problem. Just not sure it's a great idea, Lex."

"Is there something I need to know about Drake?"

"No, he seems like a good guy. Are you sure you're ready to think about dating again?"

I nodded my head. "I better be since I went to dinner with him last night, and he seems pretty persistent."

"Damn. I'm sure he is. You need anything, you come to me. You know that, right?"

"No, Jackson. If she needs something, she is going to come to me from now on," Drake said from behind me. He placed his hand on my back. "I get that you guys are friends, but she has me in her life now."

Jackson leveled Drake with a serious look. "No offense, Drake, but boyfriends come and go. I will always be part of Alexa's life and will be here for her if she ever needs me whether you like it or not. If you're going to spend time with her, then you better get used to it."

"As long as we both know where my place is and where yours is, we'll be fine," Drake responded.

I jumped into the conversation before it escalated into a fight. "Down, boys. I'm a big girl. I get to decide who is in my life and who I go to for help. Learn how to get along or it won't be either of you. Now, I'm starving. I'm going to go eat, and each of you can choose to join me or not."

Their staring contest ended as they both turned to look at me. I wasn't sure what the pissing contest was about, but I wasn't about to let it interfere in my friendship with Jackson or what was starting to develop between Drake and me. I walked to the cafe and they both followed me.

I dropped my bag onto an open table and dug through it for my Coach wristlet. Drake reached out to stop me. "Sit down. I'll grab lunch. What do you want?"

"You don't have to get my lunch," I said at the same time that Jackson chimed in with, "Grab her a turkey sandwich on sourdough with cheddar cheese, a bag of pretzels, and a Diet Coke. It's what she gets for lunch every day."

Drake didn't look very happy that Jackson had my lunch selections memorized.

"It's a funny quirk of mine. Once I find something I really like at any restaurant, it's usually the only thing I will get from there. That way, I'm not disappointed when a new dish isn't as good as my favorite."

"Manicotti at Ciao Bella, turkey sandwich here, and Moo Goo Gai Pan at Golden Wall. When you eat out with Lex, it's pretty predictable," Jackson explained, trying to push Drake's button, but it had the opposite effect.

"Let me guess, caramel swirl ice cream is another favorite? I've already hit several of them. Can't wait for the Golden Wall experience. We'll have to do that this weekend, babe."

Drake went to grab our sandwiches, and I glared at Jackson. "I thought you were starving. Shouldn't you go get your lunch?"

He glanced to where Drake stood in line. "I will in a second. Want to make one thing clear. No matter where this thing with Drake goes, you need to know I'm not going anywhere. I meant it when I said I'm here for you, Lex."

"Awww, Jackson. I know that. You are one of the reasons I didn't lose all faith in guys after what happened with Brad. I wouldn't give up our friendship for anything in this world. We'll figure it all out. Don't worry. Just give him a chance, okay?"

"Drake's a pretty intense guy, Lex. I'm not sure you're ready for a boyfriend like that. But if he's who you want, I'll give him a chance. And if he messes up, I'll be here."

"That's the pot calling the kettle black, Jackson. It's not like you're a laid-back guy either."

"Which means I know what I'm talking about. Promise me you'll take your time getting to know him. Make sure you fit together before diving into a relationship."

"Jackson, I know you worry about me, and I love you for it. But I'm not going to take relationship advice from you. You don't even have girlfriends. Just random hookups!"

"Doesn't mean I don't want one or I know how they should work. My parents set a great example, and I'm just waiting for the right girl to be ready for me." My jaw dropped as he walked away.

Drake set our trays down on the table. "Better close that mouth, babe. You're giving me ideas."

"I can't believe it. I think there's someone that Jackson is really interested in. With all the one-night stands, I never even pictured him with someone." I rubbed my hands together in glee. "Matchmaking time! I just need to figure out who it is."

Drake pulled my hands towards his mouth and kissed my palms, his tongue darting out to taste my skin. "No, babe. Leave it alone. Jackson doesn't need you to set him up."

"But what if she's perfect for him?"

"Then he would have gone after her himself. He isn't shy around the ladies. If he really wanted her, he would have done something about it."

Jackson returned to the table, so I dropped the subject and took a bite of my sandwich. "Mmmm. I don't know what it is about the sandwiches here, but I love them. Has to be the meat."

Drake and Jackson looked at each other and busted up laughing.

"Shut up! You know I didn't mean it that way. Perverts."

Their humor put a stop to the tension between the guys. They joked around while we finished our food. I watched them as I ate and hoped they would continue getting along this well if Drake became important to me. Lost in my thoughts, I didn't realize they had both finished eating until Drake snapped his fingers to get my attention.

"You going to make it through the rest of the day?" he asked me.

"Yeah, just zoned out for a minute."

"I've got to head over to my afternoon class, and I have practice tonight. Wanna come watch me play?" He wagged his eyebrows, making it seem more suggestive than watching him at rugby.

"I can't. I need to head over to the airport and make sure everything is set for the tours I have booked this week. Sorry."

Jackson snorted when I said tours since he knew it was how I referred to the Mile High Club flights in front of anyone who didn't know about them. Other than Dad, Aubrey, and her family, I didn't discuss them with anyone else except customers. Trying to explain the flights was awkward, so I avoided it as much as possible.

"Damn, that's too bad. Do you have an early class again tomorrow?" Drake asked as he gathered up our trash.

"I have an eight a.m. class every morning. I like to get them done early so I have plenty of time to study since I work most evenings during the week."

"It figures you'd be a morning person. Meet you at the dorm again tomorrow?" Drake enquired.

"Sure. If you want to get up early again, I'm not going to stop you."

He leaned over and gave me a quick peck on the lips. "See you then. I'll call you tonight when I get back to the house."

WE FELL INTO a pattern over the next couple weeks, with Drake walking me to class and eating lunch with me. We didn't have much time at night to see each other between my charter flights and his rugby team practices, but we texted and talked on the phone. I looked forward to his call each night before bed. Cuddled in safety of my bed, I felt like we could talk about anything. Weekends were jam-packed for both of us, as I had made plans with my dad and had flights booked. Drake's team was getting ready for the first rugby game at the end of the month. Even though we only saw each other during the day, we still learned so much about each other when we talked on the phone.

Friday morning rolled around, and I was thrilled to finally have some free time after classes this afternoon. I was pretty excited because Drake had mentioned that he didn't have any plans for the weekend yet. I was hoping we'd get a chance to go on another date. I must have been louder than usual getting ready because I woke Aubrey up.

"Hey, where's the fire?" she asked. "You're running around like a chicken with its head chopped off."

"No fire. Just ready for the weekend." I smiled at her as I held up two shirts for her to pick from.

"The green," she said as she pointed at the top in my left hand. "Your eyes really pop when you wear that one."

"Thanks! What would I do without your fashion advice?"

"You didn't really care what you wore until you met Drake. Glad all my knowledge is finally being put to good use for you. Big plans today?"

"Nope, just the usual. Are you going to be able to meet us for lunch today? I've barely seen you lately!"

"It's been crazy. Besides, you've been walking around with your head in the clouds with a thinking-of-Drake look on your face all the time. I'm not sure you even realized who was around you."

"Have I really been that bad?" I asked as I sat down on the bed. I never wanted Aubrey to think that she wasn't important to me.

"Nah, it's been good to see. I'm glad you're getting back on the horse. Maybe we can double date sometime."

"Drake, you, me, and what guy? Did I miss something important? New boyfriend? Spill, chica."

Aubrey laughed at my attempt with the third degree. "Nobody in particular, but a double date would be fun. We haven't been able to do one in forever. I'm sure I can rustle up a guy."

"Yeah, like that would be a problem. Just be careful 'cause you know how they fall in love with you at the slightest hint that you're interested."

Aubrey shoved me off her bed. "Like you're one to talk. Drake certainly seems smitten. Isn't he waiting downstairs for you two hours before his first class just so he can walk you across campus?"

I glanced at the clock and threw on the green shirt. "Crap! He's probably already here. I better run. See you at lunch?"

"Sure. I'll meet you at the café around noon. Now go! You don't want to keep your hottie waiting too long. I'm sure the rest of the girls are drooling over him now that they've realized he comes to get you each morning."

Aubrey was right. Word must have spread like wildfire in my dorm because a group of girls had been hanging out in the entertainment area on our floor that first Tuesday morning when I left my room. I hadn't really gotten to know most of them yet, but they all said hello to me and knew who I was.

As I headed downstairs, I could hear giggles coming from outside. It looked like Drake's fan club had become braver and weren't waiting to follow me out anymore. A couple girls were standing next to him, trying to get his attention as he glanced at the door, looking for me. He looked relieved as I stepped out. He prowled towards me with a predatory gleam in his eyes.

"Morning, babe," he said before pulling me towards him for a deep kiss. His arms wrapped around me, holding me tight as his mouth devoured mine. He bit my lower lip and growled, "Open."

My lips parted and his tongue took possession of my mouth. My body melted into his as he squeezed me tighter. He sucked on my tongue, and chills went up my spine. He gentled the kiss before pulling away and looking deep into my eyes.

"That's a hell of a way to greet me in the morning. What did I do to deserve that?" I asked.

"You deserve that and more just by being you, but I figured I should make my intentions blatantly clear. I'm here each morning because you're here. It's time everyone realized it."

I glanced over at the girls who had been trying to flirt with Drake.

They both looked at me enviously before walking away. "I think that made it pretty obvious. Maybe they'll tell all their friends and word will spread through your whole fan club."

"And maybe I need to do that again when some of the guys who want you are around."

"What guys?" I asked.

"Nope. Carry on being clueless to other men. You don't need to worry about any guy except me."

He walked me to my morning class like usual but stopped me outside the building instead of coming inside. Before I realized what he meant to do, he gave me another deep kiss. When he was done, he flashed me a smug grin. "See you at lunch."

As he walked away, I saw him stop to talk to a group of his frat brothers. One of them glanced my way and smiled. Drake shoved him to the side and stood between us without looking back at me. Crazy boy. I shook my head at his antics and went to class.

Drake was waiting for me at a table in the café when I got there for lunch. He'd already gotten me my usual, and he was chatting with Aubrey. It was nice to see them getting along so well. Aubrey's opinion mattered a lot to me.

"Hey," I greeted them as I sat down. "Thanks for grabbing my lunch again. One of these days, I'll beat you here so I can buy for a change."

Drake shook his head. "Not gonna happen."

"What? I can't pay for lunch?"

"Nope. That's not how this works. You need something and I'm with you, then I buy it for you."

"Drake, that's ridiculous," I argued.

"Not to me, babe. Don't make that big of a deal out of it. Feeding you isn't going to break the bank."

I looked at Aubrey, expecting her to back me up. She just shrugged her shoulders in a gesture of helplessness. "What? You agree with him?"

"No, but you should pick your battles. Does it really bother you that you have a drop-dead gorgeous guy who wants to be a gentleman when he takes you out?"

I glared at her. "Geesh, when you put it that way, I sound like a whiny bitch. Thanks a lot for the help here."

"Wouldn't matter if she agreed with you, Alexa. There's nothing for her to back you up on. You know me by now. Can you picture me letting you pay on a date?"

I shook my head no since I really couldn't. "You're such a Neanderthal sometimes."

"Yeah, but I'm yours." He winked at me. "Speaking of dates, I made plans for us tonight. I haven't had you to myself all week."

Aubrey clapped her hands together. "Oooh, a guy who plans your dates and pays for them. I like the sound of that! Where are you guys going?"

"I want it to be a surprise," Drake answered.

"I'm not really good with surprises."

"She isn't. The anticipation always gets to her as she imagines the worst," Aubrey agreed.

"Don't worry. I promise you're going to like this one. I'll pick you up at eight."

"Are you sure you don't just want to tell me what we're doing? I can't promise that I won't worry about it all day."

Drake's gaze turned serious. "Alexa, trust me when I tell you that you've got nothing to be concerned about. If you don't like my plans, I'll change them. Okay?"

I pouted up at him and batted my eyelashes.

"Enough with the puppy-dog look. I'm not telling you what I have planned. Gotta run or I'll be late for class. See you at eight."

He strode away from the table, and Aubrey chuckled next to me. "What's so funny?"

"I think he'll be good for you in more ways than I thought. I don't think I've ever seen you back down so quickly from trying to spoil a surprise. Maybe he'll break you of that habit so I can actually hide your Christmas present from you this year."

"I'm not that bad, Aubrey."

"Um, yeah, you are. Why do you think I always cave and give you presents early? If I shop in advance for you, it's a wasted trip because I can never hold out. Where do you think half the clothes I give you come from?"

"Your closet? Or an impulse buy while you're out shopping for yourself?"

Aubrey made a buzzing sound. "Wrong answer. But I don't really mind. So, date night. Are you excited?"

"Yeah, I am. Will you meet me at the dorm to help me get ready? Maybe you have a gift waiting in your closet for me right now that will be perfect for tonight?" I joked.

"No such luck. We'll have to make do with what you've already got on hand. See you later."

Chapter 9

A S I DRESSED for our big date, Aubrey popped into the room to check on me. "So what's the plan for tonight? Still no idea where Drake's taking you?"

"Nope. I tried again to talk him into spilling the beans, but it's still a surprise. He just said that I needed to wear jeans. What do you think?" I asked her as I gestured down at my outfit. I had chosen to wear a pair of dark blue jeans with a deep green sweater and brown leather boots. The jeans were snug but not super tight. The sweater hit mid-thigh but clung to my boobs. The boots were a favorite of mine, with only a slight heel on them. I felt comfortable but hoped I still looked good for Drake.

"Turn around," Aubrey instructed as she made a circle motion. "I can't make a judgment call on the outfit until I can see it all."

I twirled around and did a little bow as I faced her again. "Well? Will I do?"

Aubrey clapped her hands together. "Yes! You look great. You're gonna knock his socks off. Not that it's his socks that you really want to knock off, right?"

"Ha-ha, funny. You know how much I hate feet, so that would be a big fat no."

"And you know that wasn't the point I was trying to make. I swear at lunch today, I felt like I could get pregnant just from being an innocent bystander to the sexual vibes you guys were throwing off," Aubrey said as she fanned herself. "You need to do something about that before one of you spontaneously combusts."

"Oh my God, I cannot believe that you just said that. That's a big step. Do you really think I'm ready to have sex with Drake? Isn't it too early? I haven't really known him that long," I asked.

Aubrey shrugged her shoulders. "I don't know. You're the only one who can answer that question for yourself. But I can tell you that it's going to happen sooner or later. There is no way that you won't end up in bed with Drake at some point in time. He wants you badly, and you eat him up with your eyes every time he walks into a room. Hell, your eyes get all dreamy whenever you mention his name. Admit it—you're already falling for him."

"I really am, Aubrey, and it scares the shit out of me." I crossed my arms across my stomach for comfort.

"It's okay to be scared. You just can't let fear make your decisions for you. You don't let fear rule you when you're piloting a plane. Don't do it with this relationship either." Aubrey came over and wrapped me into a hug. "What's the worst thing that could happen when you're in the air?"

"The plane could crash and I could die," I snapped back at her.

"And if Drake breaks your heart?" she asked.

"I don't know. If I fall any deeper, it would hurt so bad that I might wish I was dead."

Aubrey leveled me with a serious look. "Not gonna happen. Not with me here to help pick up the pieces. Flying is much scarier than falling in love because the risks are bigger. You're just used to those risks. The only way you're going to get used to them in relationships is if you give this a real chance. No holding yourself back. Really try to make this work with Drake. As scary as it is to think about having sex with only the second person in your life, it's better to take the plunge with someone you're starting to care for than to go out and have a string of one-night stands, right?"

There was some logic in her twisted reasoning. If I was going to get back on the horse, so to speak, then it would be better to be with someone within a relationship than participate in the random hookups that happened every day on campus. "I hear what you're saying, and I'll try my best to not freak out tonight if things go down that path. But I don't know that they will. Drake is being very careful not to push too hard with me."

Aubrey squeezed me and stepped away. "That's easily solved. Just let him know that you're ready to take it to the next level with him. Trust me when I say that he won't hesitate for a second. I can tell from the way he watches you. You've got good underwear on just in case?"

I giggled. "Yes, and I shaved too 'cause I know that's you're next question."

"Then it sounds like you've already made the decision before my little pep talk. You skip the undies and shaving when you don't plan on having sex. It's good protection to stop yourself from getting naked. But if you've prepped for the date, then you're already picturing yourself having sex with him."

I nodded in agreement. "I know. You taught me well, Obi-Wan Kenobi."

I heard a knock at the door and rushed into the other room to answer it. I needed to see Drake now to help settle my nerves. It sounded crazy because of the butterflies I felt every time I saw him, but he made me feel safe when we were together. I opened the door, and there he was. I felt the air leave my lungs in a rush of relief.

"Hi," I greeted him.

"Hey, babe," he replied as he snaked an arm out to pull me into his body. His mouth swooped down and claimed mine for a quick kiss. "You ready?"

"Yeah. Let me grab my purse and then we can head out." I turned back toward my room to grab what I needed, but Aubrey was waiting behind me with my purse in hand.

"Here you go. I threw a couple things in there that I thought you might need," she said as she winked at me. "Hi, Drake. Hope you guys have fun tonight. Make sure you take good care of my girl."

"Don't worry, Aubrey. I always take very good care of my girl," he growled at us. "Right, baby?"

I nodded, and Aubrey handed me my purse. I peeked inside and discovered that she had stocked it with a clean pair of panties, condoms, and gum. I raised shocked eyes to her and she flashed me a huge grin as she shooed us out of the room.

Drake's car wasn't waiting at the curb like usual. In its place was a gleaming black Harley. "You own a motorcycle?"

He shook his head. "Not mine. I borrowed it from a buddy. Wanted to take you for a ride, feel your body wrapped around me. You ever been on one before?"

"Sure have. Jackson has one. His dad loves 'em. It's been a couple years though."

"Then you know the drill," he said as he handed me a helmet off the back. "Hop on."

Riding behind Drake was very different from riding with Jackson when I was younger. I wrapped my arms around his body and held on tight as we took off. My breasts pushed against his back, and my nipples pebbled in reaction. My thighs were wrapped outside of his. I could feel his muscles ripple as he controlled the bike. The heat from his body radiated through his clothes as I hugged him even closer and wiggled in my seat a little.

His hand tugged one of mine lower, away from his abdomen. Our hands brushed against his hard cock before he placed my hand on his thigh. He groaned in response as I squeezed his leg. "It's a good thing we aren't going very far. I underestimated how good it feels to have you snuggled against me. Need to be careful since I have precious cargo on board."

I relaxed against him and enjoyed the feel of the bike rumbling beneath me. As we drove into town, I quickly guessed our destination. "Golden Wall? Yummy!"

"Wanted to enjoy another of your favorites with you tonight."

"Best Chinese food in town and the best guy around. I'm a lucky girl."

"I'm the lucky one, Alexa. I know you weren't sure about giving me a chance. Hope this last week has shown you that I'm worth the risk."

He pulled the bike into a parking spot next to the restaurant and waited for me to get off before placing the kickstand. I handed him the helmet and ran my fingers through my hair to fix it.

"You look great, Alexa. Don't worry about your hair. Makes you look like we just rolled out of bed."

"Helmet head is different from bed head, Drake."

"Here's hoping I find that out for myself soon," he said as we walked into the restaurant.

I waited until we were seated before responding. "Maybe you won't have to hope much longer. I don't think I want to wait anymore."

"Babe, shit. You can't say stuff like that before we've even ordered our meal. Fuck! How am I going to make it through dinner? Are you sure?"

"100% sure, no. It's been a long time for me, but you're driving me crazy!"

"I'm not gonna take you until you're ready to commit to me, but there's lots of other stuff I can do to tide both of us over until you're ready."

"Drake," I sighed. The waiter appeared at our table as I gazed pleadingly at him.

His eyes held mine as he spoke. "I'm sorry, but something's come up. Could we get a couple drinks and order our food to go?"

Drake ordered himself a beer and a glass of white wine for me. The waiter didn't ask for identification, and I was grateful for the shot of courage the alcohol would provide. When the waiter brought us our drinks, he ordered a few different menu items for us to take with us. He pulled his phone out and focused on the screen for a few minutes before nodding in satisfaction.

Drake's heated gaze rested on me as he sipped his beer. I nervously gulped my wine, feeling anxious all of the sudden. "Nothing to fear with me, Alexa. I'll take good care of you, I swear."

"It's just nerves. I wouldn't have said anything if I didn't trust you to some degree already."

"We'll only go as far as I think you're ready. No sex tonight, babe. But I promise to take the edge off for you."

The waiter came back with our food, and Drake handed him his credit card. He must have thought it was an emergency with how quickly the food was prepared. He returned with the slip for Drake to sign in less than a minute, and we were on our way out the door. Drake put the bag of food into the saddlebag on the side, and we roared out of the parking lot as soon as I was settled behind him. I quickly realized that we weren't headed back towards campus though.

"Where are we going?" I asked.

"Not gonna spend my first night with you in a frat house or at your dorm," he replied as he pulled into the parking lot of the Hyatt Place.

"You booked us a hotel room?"

"Wasn't what I had planned for tonight, but that's what online reservations were made for. Booked it as soon as I realized you were mine tonight."

I felt strange as we checked into the hotel without any luggage, just a bag of Chinese food. The clerk didn't seem to notice anything amiss and handed Drake our keycard. I turned away as he gave Drake directions to our room. My face had heated with the blush that had crept up my neck.

We stopped at the vending machine to grab a couple sodas on our way to the room. Drake opened the door and waved me in ahead of him. I flipped the light switch and my eyes locked on the king-sized bed that dominated the room.

Drake rubbed his hand down my back in a soothing gesture. "Nothing has to happen tonight, Alexa. We can spread out with our food and watch television if that's what you want to do."

"You and me, alone in a hotel room, without anything happening? I don't think so."

He took a couple towels from the bathroom and spread them across the bed. Pulling containers out of the bag, he peeked inside each one and handed me the Moo Goo Gai Pan with a fork.

"What, no chopsticks?"

He dug through the bag some more and pulled out a set that he tossed my way. He watched as I pulled them out of the packaging and used them to scoop some food into my mouth. His eyes lingered on my lips as I chewed. The air in the room sizzled with sexual tension as we sat across from each other and ate silently. Our fingers brushed as we both reached for an eggroll and I froze.

"You first," Drake offered, handing me the bag.

"No thanks. I think I'm full." I rubbed my stomach, which was fluttering like crazy. I couldn't possibly eat anything else as my nerves were getting the best of me.

Drake took a bite of an eggroll and started clearing up the mess. I leapt off the bed, grabbed the mostly full containers, and tossed them into the garbage can.

Drake handed me a small toiletry kit stamped with the Hyatt name. "How did you get this?"

"The guy at the check-in desk must have thought we might need it. He slid it over to me while he was checking out your ass and gave me the thumbs-up sign."

"Ohimigod! That's so embarrassing."

"We aren't the first couple to show up spur of the moment and I'm sure we won't be the last. Go get ready for bed. There should be a couple robes in the closet. Why don't you change into one of them?"

As I brushed my teeth, I took deep breathes to try to calm my nerves. It was my idea to spend the night with Drake, and here I was, trembling like a schoolgirl. I'd only ever been naked in front of one other guy. I had no doubts that Drake was attracted to me, so I really didn't have anything to be worried about. I just needed to pull up my big girl panties and walk out there. I could do this.

Dressed in the robe with just my underwear on, I stepped out of the bathroom. Drake was already undressed and in his robe. He gave me a reassuring look as he stepped past me to use the bathroom. The lights were dimmed and the television was on and turned to the movies that were available to purchase. I flipped through the options and found several action films I hadn't caught at the theater. I clicked on the preview for the one starring Jason Statham, since he was my favorite actor.

The blankets were already turned down, so I climbed into the bed. I heard the water turn off in the bathroom and glanced towards the door to see Drake staring at me. "I like the look of you in bed waiting for me."

He stalked towards me and climbed in beside me. He towered over me on his knees as he looked down at me. His eyes darkened as he trailed them down my body and back up again to look me in the eyes. His jaw was clenched and his cheeks flushed. I could practically feel the testosterone pumping into the air. He glanced to the side to look at the television.

"Good choice in movies. No chick flick?" he joked in an effort to diffuse the tension.

I punched him in the arm as he settled next to me, pulling me into his side. "No, I love action movies. My tastes must have been influenced by my dad's preferences since he raised me on his own."

Drake gave me a reassuring squeeze. "He did a great job with you, babe."

"It was hard on him losing Mom like he did when she had me, but he was a great dad."

"Wasn't easy for you either growing up without a mom. He never thought about remarrying?"

I shook my head. "He's dated some throughout the years, but never anything serious. He always said Mom was the love of his life, and he couldn't imagine replacing her."

"If you're anything like your mom, I think I understand what he meant." My heart raced at the words he'd said so casually. "Enough serious talk for tonight. I want to enjoy our time together. This the movie you want to watch?"

"Yes, please," I whispered.

He hit the purchase button, and the movie began to play. It was the third in a series I loved, and I quickly found myself sucked into it. I rested my head on Drake's chest, and his hands combed through my hair as we watched the movie. It was action-packed, and Jason Statham had several shirtless scenes. Drake's hand moved down my back, rubbing lightly. Goose bumps raised everywhere he touched as my breath sped up. By the time the movie was over, I was practically panting with need.

My robe had slid partway off my shoulders, and Drake was caressing the back of my neck. I'd opened the front of his robe so my cheek was pressed against his skin. I could hear his heart beating thunderously, and I pressed a kiss into his chest. He groaned loudly and rolled me onto my back. I pulled his mouth down to my mine and kissed him. He moaned hungrily as our mouths danced together, exploring each other.

I was throbbing with need, and I moved my legs restlessly. Drake broke our kiss and worked his way down my body with his lips. His tongue flicked over one of my nipples as his fingers rolled the other. He sucked hard and I felt the pull deep inside. I arched my back, trying to get closer.

"Oh, God!" I whimpered.

"Shh, baby. I've got you," Drake murmured against my skin. His mouth moved to the other nipple, and he bit down gently. His hands pressed me against the bed as his lips moved down my stomach, nibbling his way across my skin. His tongue teased my belly button, sending a zing through me. His hands swept farther down, caressing my legs. They spread as he moved over me.

He held my hips, and I felt his breath through my panties. He kissed around the edges, licking the seams of my pussy. I could feel moisture dripping from me, drenching my panties. His finger lightly teased over my folds, finding the dampness.

"Lift up, Alexa," he said as he tugged my panties down my legs.

He kissed his way back up my body until his tongue, soft and gentle, lapped at my pussy lips. "Fucking beautiful," he whispered. "You're so wet for me, baby."

His fingers spread me open, and he ran his tongue up and down my clit. My world nearly dissolved at the feel of his warm mouth on me. His thumb pressed against me, slowly sliding inside. I threw my head back against the pillows and moaned deeply. He stopped, his mouth hovering over me. "No, please. Don't stop," I moaned.

"Watch me, baby. I want your eyes on me while you come. Need to see you fly apart."

I struggled to keep my eyes open as his tongue flicked out and stroked my clit. I plunged my hands into his hair, praying he wouldn't stop. He buried his tongue deep inside me, driving me out of my mind with need before he replaced it with two fingers. They moved slowly as he rubbed against my g-spot. I could feel a climax starting to build, and then he wrapped his lips around my clit and sucked hard. I screamed as the climax hit my body. I held his head to me as I ground my hips against his mouth.

My body relaxed as all the tension left me. My body was covered in a fine sheen of sweat as Drake gently licked me until I calmed. He moved over me and licked his lips before kissing me. I could taste myself on him, and he groaned as my tongue flicked against his.

"Never seen anything as beautiful as that, Alexa."

"What about you?" I asked, glancing down at his lap where the robe was tented by his hard-on.

"This was about you, baby. I've been hard for you since the day we met. It isn't going to kill me," he said as he reached down to adjust himself.

The sight of his hand shifting his hardened cock made my clit throb again. I reached out and pressed his hand against it. "If you won't let me help, let me watch."

Drake's head snapped up, and he looked at me in shock. "Alexa, wait. This isn't what tonight is about."

"Please, Drake. You got to watch me come. I want to see, too. Don't make me beg."

His eyes flared as his self-control snapped. He leaned over and kissed me, hard and deep. Then he lay back on the pillows and opened his robe. I gasped as I saw his exposed cock for the first time. He fisted the hardened length with his hand, and it stood thick and proud. A drop of pre-cum glistened at the tip, and I licked my lips, aching to taste him.

I couldn't breathe. Drake slicked pre-cum over the head of his cock before moving his hand up and down. I was more turned on than I had ever been in my life while watching his fist stroking his cock.

"God, you're so fucking beautiful. Yes, watch me, baby."

My gaze flew to his face, mesmerized by the pleasure I saw. "I couldn't look away if I tried, Drake."

My legs squeezed together, giving myself a little bit of relief from the ache the sight of him masturbating caused. "Alexa," he moaned my name. I whimpered as he came, spurting ropes of cum onto his chest.

"Jesus, Drake. That was the hottest thing I've ever seen."

"No, watching you come and knowing it was because of me is even hotter."

He grabbed a towel from the floor and wiped himself off. I pulled my robe tight around me, a little overwhelmed by what had just happened between us now that the intensely hot moment had passed. Drake must have sensed the shift in my mood because he pulled me tight against him and kissed the top of my head.

"I pushed too hard, didn't I?" he asked huskily, regret coloring his tone.

I closed my eyes tightly as I buried my head in his chest. "No! Not at all, Drake. Spending the night together was my idea in the first place. It's just a little strange is all. Things have never progressed this fast for me before."

He rubbed circles on my back in an effort to settle my nerves. "Look at me, baby."

I tilted my head upwards and opened my eyes just enough to peek at him. "What?" I whispered.

"You never need to be embarrassed with me. What happens in bed between us is hot as shit, but it's also fucking beautiful. That was a little taste of how it's going to be with us. When you're ready for more, we're gonna burn up the sheets. Just want you to get comfortable with me for now. I hadn't even planned on it going this far tonight, but fuck if I could stop myself. Not sure how I'm gonna do it, but I promise you I'll have more self-control next time."

I peered deep into his eyes, seeing his determination to give me what he thought I needed. I reached up and cupped his cheek. "Drake, that isn't what I meant. Yeah, I'm a little uncomfortable now, but it's mostly because I don't have a lot of experience with guys. I've only had one serious boyfriend, and things ended badly between us. It's been a while, so this is all new to me."

His eyes flared at the mention of a previous boyfriend. "Don't really want to think about the other guys you've been with. I know we both have pasts, but you're mine now, baby."

I giggled a little at his possessive words. "I know it's not really what I am supposed to do, lying here in bed with you, but you have to know something. There's only ever been the one other guy. No worries there."

He squeezed me even tighter. "Wish I could have been your first, but I'll work my hardest to make sure I'm your last. Can't say that there haven't been a fuck of a lot more women in my bed than guys you've been with. I've never had something like this. And I don't want to lose it."

"Those are pretty strong words this fast, don't you think?"

"I know special when I see it, Alexa. Not many women out there are hot, sweet, smart, and funny. And the fucking chemistry between us. I'd be an idiot not to know that I found something you don't find every day. Hell, that some people will never find."

I blushed at his praise as my eyes started drifting shut. I was starting to crash after the surge of adrenaline, and the warmth of Drake's body added to his hand stroking my back was making it hard to keep my eyes open. "Mmmmmm," I mumbled.

"Your body needed that climax, baby. Look at you all flushed and satisfied. Go ahead, close your eyes and go to sleep."

Drake's voice murmuring to me was the last thing I remembered before I slipped into a deep slumber. I'd never spent the whole night in bed with a guy before, but I slept better than I had in ages. His body stayed curled around mine, one arm thrown over me and a leg tucked between my thighs.

I USUALLY AWOKE with the sun each morning, and the next day was no exception. I was disoriented at first, not recognizing the room and the feel of Drake next to me. My eyes blinked open as I took a deep breath and found his scent surrounding me. Yesterday's events came rushing back to me. I looked over at Drake only to find him staring down at me.

"Were you watching me sleep? That's a little bit creepy, isn't it?" I teased.

Drake's husky chuckle sent shivers up my spine. "Just woke up. Happy to find you next to me. Fucking great way to start the morning."

"It is nice to wake up with you. Thought you weren't a morning person?"

"Never have been before. You were a little restless before you woke up. I felt you moving next to me."

"I'm so sorry! Go back to sleep. I'll hop in the shower while you rest some more."

His eyes heated as he glanced down to the opening at the top of the robe. It had parted, the tops of my breasts visible. "Not a chance in this world that I'd be able to go back to sleep with you naked in a shower this close to me."

"Well don't expect me to invite you into my shower time, bucko. I take my showers very seriously."

His finger trailed over the top of my breasts. "You sure about that? I could wash your back for you."

"I'm pretty sure washing my back would be the last thing on either of our minds if you got in the shower with me."

He leaned in for a kiss, and I wrapped my hand over my mouth since I hadn't brushed my teeth yet. Undeterred, he dropped light kisses on my neck instead and moved towards the opening of the robe. I gently nudged his head away as I scooted off the bed. He lay there, the sheet draped over him, with his robe nowhere in sight. He looked like a sex god with his hair tousled and a sexy gleam in his eyes.

"Promise I'll be good," he said as he crossed his fingers and put them behind his back in an exaggerated movement.

"Good at being bad? That doesn't count," I tossed over my shoulder as I walked into the bathroom and shut the door. If I looked at him, even for a second more, I was going to cave and beg him to join me. He was just too damn tempting. I heard his deep laugh through the door and locked it for good measure.

The robe dropped to the floor, and I saw a trail of light red marks he'd left on my body with his nips and nibbles. They were barely visible, but the sight of them thrilled me in an unexpected way. Sex with Brad had been good, but that didn't even compare to last night with Drake. If he could make me feel this way with just oral, then what was I in for when we went all the way?

I hurried through my shower. I wouldn't be surprised if Drake found a way into the bathroom if I wasn't quick about it. He was definitely going to be a bad influence while keeping me on my toes. As I finished up, I heard footsteps by the door, followed by a loud thunk.

"Drake? Everything okay out there?"

"No, help. I'm dying out here," he groaned in response.

I threw the robe on and pulled the door open, only to find him standing there staring at me. "What's wrong? Are you hurt?"

"I couldn't handle it any longer. The sound of running water, knowing it was hitting your naked body. Thank fuck, you put me out of my misery. It won't even matter if you used all the hot water 'cause I'm going to need the longest cold shower ever."

I busted up laughing. "Ohmigosh, Drake! You had me thinking you were at death's door. Don't scare me like that again."

"I make no promises. You might as well tie me down if you're ever going to subject me to the torture of listening to you shower again without letting me join you."

"Watch it, buster. If you aren't careful, I'll tie you to a chair and put you in the bathroom with me so you can look and hear without touching."

"Don't threaten me with a good time, baby. The view would be worth some pain."

"Pain? I'll give you pain." I swatted him on his butt. "You better hurry up and get ready. I'm starving. Feed me!"

"Let me guess. Pancakes?"

"Pretty please with sugar on top."

"How about you give me some sugar instead?" Drake said, tapping his lips with his fingertips.

I reached up to give him a quick kiss and then danced out of his reach. "Ah, ah, ah. Shower time."

As Drake took his shower, I rummaged through my purse to see what toiletries I had on hand for this morning. I'm not sure how she managed it, but Aubrey had squeezed a matching set of bra and panties, a small cosmetics bag, and an extra top in there along with the condoms she'd thrown inside last night. What a relief! No walk-of-shame look for me today.

By the time Drake strolled out of the bathroom—with nothing on but a towel wrapped around his lean hips—I was dressed and ready to go. He had showered fast and looked disappointed when he realized I was done getting ready. I watched, unable to look away, as a bead of water rolled down his naked chest. His hand reached for the knot in the towel, and I jerked my eyes up to his face. He was smirking at me, delighted to have caught me ogling him.

"Go ahead. Do it. Drop the towel. I dare you!" I teased, playing along.

Drake's eyes flared as he cocked his head at me. He took several steps in my direction before pulling the knot loose and letting the towel fall. I fought hard to keep my eyes locked with his instead of looking down. If I did, I knew I'd be a goner and we wouldn't make it out the door for breakfast. I truly was starving, and I could use a little bit of distance this morning. Things were moving so quickly, and the feelings he evoked in me were too powerful.

"You afraid to look, baby?" he taunted me.

I slapped my hands over my face, covering my eyes to help resist the temptation he presented. "Nope. Not gonna work, Drake."

"Nerves of steel, huh? Fine, I'll throw my clothes on and we'll head out to breakfast. Party pooper!"

I threw my stuff back into my purse, barely getting it to all fit. By the time Drake was dressed, I'd checked the room to make sure we weren't leaving anything behind. As we left the room, I turned to look back. I had a feeling Drake had just made the Hyatt Place my favorite hotel with the memory of our first sexual encounter etched in my mind. He'd left me wanting more, too, damn him!

Drake took me to a local hole-in-the-wall diner that served amazing breakfasts. As we walked in, I recognized several people at tables enjoying their Saturday morning. They were all friends of my dad, so I was sure that I'd be hearing from him later today when word got back that I'd been spotted here with Drake this early. And this is why looking presentable had been so important this morning. If I had combined my outfit from yesterday with bed head and no mascara, I'd have a hard time explaining to my dad what was going on. Now I could just say we'd met for breakfast without worrying that Dad would know I'd been doing the walk of shame. Yet another thing for which Aubrey deserved my thanks.

"How is it that you seem to know someone everywhere we go?" Drake asked as the waitress placed the food on the table.

"When you grow up in a college town this size, you get to know just about everybody. Plus, Aubrey's family owns the local bank so they literally know everyone. We've been best friends forever, so I pretty much know anyone she does, too. A lot of people know me through her."

"I like how you and Aubrey are so tight. You seem so different from each other, but you fit together as friends."

"She's awesome! I really lucked out in the best friend department. How about you? It had to have been hard transferring here as a junior and leaving your friends behind."

Drake shrugged his shoulders. "Yeah, but I can hang out with the guys on the team or from the frat. Most of them seem cool enough.

I've hung out with the team captain, Zach, a few times after practice. He wanted to make sure I was fitting in okay, I guess."

"And Jackson? How are things between you guys at the house? You've been getting along when I'm around you both."

He reached out and grabbed my hand that was playing around with my silverware. "Alexa, don't worry about Jackson and me. We're getting along fine. He gets where I'm going with you, and I know where he stands with you."

"I just need you guys to be okay, that's all. He's the closest thing I have to a brother, and you're becoming important to me."

"Baby, the last thing I want to do is mess up your friendship with Jackson. I know what he means to you. Won't say that it isn't a little hard for me to swallow knowing how close you are to him, but I get it. I'll try to tone down my caveman tendencies when it comes to him, but not with any other guy."

I giggled in response. "You don't have to worry. There is no other guy, and Jackson really isn't a guy. He's just Jackson."

"You keep thinking about him like that, and I won't have any problems with Jackson. Okay?"

"Deal! I can totally agree to that," I smiled across at him. "So, how's your breakfast? Mine is yummy!" I gestured to his plate, wanting to change the subject and break some of the tension.

"Great omelet. Don't know how you can get by without any protein in the morning." He shook his head as he looked at my plate of pancakes.

"Hey, there are eggs in here, too!"

"Barely. Want some of mine?" he asked as he scooped up a forkful of omelet.

"Um, no thanks. See how hidden the egg is in my pancakes? So that you don't really know they're in there? That's how I like my eggs. Yuck!"

He took a big bite and moaned in appreciation. "No eggs for you then. I guess that means I'll have to learn how to make pancakes."

I clapped my hands together in excitement. "Now that's more like it! I can even teach you how to make them, too."

"Works for me. We'll do that sometime. I like the thought of you in the kitchen showing me how to make something you love to eat."

I practically melted into a puddle at his sweet words and the hot look he sent my way. "Me too."

"Anything you need to do today?"

"Nope, I'm all yours for the day."

"Baby, you're not just mine for the day. You're mine period. I've had a taste of you now. Not letting you get away."

Shivers went up my spine at his possessive tone. I looked down at my plate and sighed. I didn't want to encourage his pushiness, but I knew he could tell it got to me. I never thought I'd be the type of girl to get all mushy inside when a guy turned all alpha on me, but I guess I was wrong. Drake was quickly working his way past all my defenses. In an odd sort of way, I felt safe with him because he was so upfront with his bossiness and he let me know that he felt jealous when other guys were around. How could I not be affected when he made me feel so wanted?

Chapter 10

D RAKE MUST HAVE been serious when he'd said our night together made me his because he certainly acted like it after. He wasn't shy of PDA, kissing me all the time and touching me whenever and wherever he pleased. I knew I should probably be offended by his behavior, but I found myself turned on even more. After Brad had cheated on me in such a public way, I'd felt like it had to have been my fault. He'd been my first and only lover, so I figured that I just wasn't desirable enough to keep his attention. Drake blew that negativity out of my head by showing me daily that he wanted me. Heck, he made it pretty damn clear to everyone that he wanted me. Everyone but that girl from the frat party, at least.

She didn't live in my dorm, but you'd think she did with how often we saw her in the mornings when Drake stopped by to pick me up for our walk across campus. I never saw him treat her any differently than any of the other girls who still tried to gain his attention, but she seemed to think she was special. I would usually find her standing closer to him than anyone else, talking with her hands, and using that as an excuse to touch him. It drove me crazy, not knowing what had happened between them. I understood that he had a past, but I would have preferred it to be dead and buried instead of in my face every day.

A couple months into our relationship, I finally discovered what their relationship had been before I met Drake. As I walked up to them leaving the dorm, I glanced at her hand patting his arm as she tried to keep his attention. Drake wasn't even watching her. His eyes were on me, devouring me as I neared. "Morning, baby," he greeted me with a small smile on his face that pissed me off even more.

I didn't find anything funny about this situation, and his smug grin was about to buy him a load of trouble he wasn't expecting this morning. I'd taken about as much as I was going to from this girl, regardless of their past relationship. If our roles were reversed, he wouldn't put up with this shit. He'd just beat the crap out of the guy and pull me away.

I pointedly looked at her hand and then back to his face as I stood next to them with my arms crossed, not saying a word. Drake swatted her hand away and looked back at me with an amused expression on his face, shrugging his shoulders as if to ask what he could do about it. Arrogant bastard.

The blond girl barely registered the fact that he'd rebuffed her as she gazed up at him adoringly. "Ugh! I think I just threw up in my mouth a little," I muttered under my breath. At Drake's chuckle, I realized I hadn't said that as quietly as I'd thought. His laughter earned him a death stare from me.

"Sasha, you've met my girlfriend before," he said as he pulled me closer. "Alexa, I think you know Sasha. Our families are close since our moms are best friends."

"Really? How nice for you both," I said sarcastically as he began to unravel the mystery of how they knew each other.

Sasha looked down at our entwined fingers and then back up at Drake's face with an irritated expression. Her eyes trailed over his chest hungrily on the way up. Yay, what a good morning for me. I got to watch as a close family friend ogled my boyfriend. Yippee. She finally acknowledged my presence by looking at me like I was a bug she'd like to squash under her foot.

"Yes, it's great to have so much in common with such a great guy. I can't wait to see your family over the holidays, Drake," she said as she sent a triumphant smile my way.

Drake ran his hand up and down my back in a comforting gesture and pressed a kiss to my forehead. "Mom's excited about her annual open house. I may not be around much. Depends on what plans Alexa has. Wouldn't want to spend our first holiday apart."

Sasha's jaw dropped at his words. Our expressions of shock probably mirrored each other since Drake and I hadn't talked about plans for the holiday breaks yet. Thanksgiving was just around the corner, and it was my favorite day of the year. We usually had dinner with Aubrey's family, and I spent the night before at her house so I could help her mom start cooking early in the morning. Turkey with all the trimmings, the Macy's parade on TV, and football filled my memories of Thanksgiving each year.

Jumping on the chance to drive Sasha crazy, I leaned up to kiss Drake and whispered to him, "Childhood friends? You are so going to pay for this later." I turned my head and raised my voice so she could hear me. "I'd hate to be apart too, sweetie," I cooed.

"But, Drake, your mom would be crushed if you didn't come home for the holidays," Sasha protested.

Drake moved behind me and wrapped both arms around me, resting his chin on the top of my head. "Didn't say I wasn't going to be there. Just that my plans depend on what Alexa wants to do."

I chuckled in response and pulled his arms even tighter around my body. "That shouldn't be such a surprise, Sasha. Isn't that what good boyfriends do? And Drake really is the best."

Her nose scrunched up in distaste as she heaved a big sigh. "Whatever," she huffed as she stomped away.

Drake turned me so that we were now facing each other. "Damn, you're so fucking hot when you're jealous."

I slapped his arm. "Jealous! What the hell, Drake? She practically stalks you around campus, and the first time I saw you, you were having an argument with her. I figured she was an ex-girlfriend and couldn't figure out why you let her hang around so much."

He rubbed his arm where I hit him, acting like it had actually hurt and pouting down at me. "You should've just asked me about her, babe."

"Argh! You are so frustrating! What was I supposed to say? 'Drake, you know that blond chick that likes to trail after you all the time and flirt? Did you just fuck her or was she your girlfriend before me?' No, wait. That wouldn't even have been specific enough 'cause there are just so many damn blondes on campus that flirt with you all the time."

Clearly not fearing the laser-beam glare I was now sending his way, Drake started to chuckle deeply. "Alexa, I'd only been on campus a few days before I noticed you. Couldn't get you out of my head, and there wasn't enough time for me to have a girlfriend and dump her for you."

I stomped my foot in frustration, not sure exactly why I was getting so angry. The Sasha mystery had been solved, and I didn't have to think about them in bed together anymore which had been driving me a little crazy with how much we bumped into her all the time. This had been building up inside all this time.

"You could have just shared with me that you knew her because your parents are friends, Drake."

"Baby, you could have asked me if it was bothering you. I figured you knew you don't have anything to worry about with Sasha. She's just a pest that I put up with 'cause our moms are friends. It didn't even cross my mind that I had anything to explain about her. Thought it was pretty clear that I'm not into her with how I act around her."

Arms crossed, I started to tap my foot. "I didn't think you liked her now, Drake. But it wasn't clear to me why you tolerated her so much. Now I get it, okay?"

He pulled my arms away from my body and wrapped them around his instead. "You gotta talk to me if something's bothering you. I'm not a mind reader. Didn't realize she got to you that much. I'll make sure she backs off from now on."

I snuggled into him, relieved that he understood why I was so upset. "You're right. I should have asked you about her before. I just didn't know what to say, and I wasn't sure that I wanted to hear the answer."

"You've got nothing to fear with me, Alexa. If this is going to work, you have to talk to me when something bothers you this much. No keeping shit inside like this anymore, got it?"

I nodded my head. "I'll try."

"Hate to tell you this, but you're late for class now."

"Crap. How late?" I asked as I jumped away from him.

"No way you're gonna make it there in time. Class already started," he said, pulling me close again. "Wanna ditch with me? Making it through our first argument calls for something special. Not a day full of boring classes."

"I can't skip all day, but I could miss my first class since I'm already late."

"Come back to the house with me?" he asked.

I gulped in response to the heat in his smoldering gaze. "Yes," I whispered.

He flashed me a triumphant grin before we headed off in the direction of his fraternity. It was strange to walk into the house early in the morning. Some of the guys were downstairs eating breakfast when we walked in. Drake nodded at them and pulled me towards the stairs. I could hear their laughter as we headed up and felt a little embarrassed that they all assumed we were going to his room for sex.

Drake's room was fairly neat for a guy, but the covers were pulled down on his bed. The sheets were rumpled, and I could see the indent his head had left on his pillow. I could picture him sprawled in his bed last night as he'd slept. Naked. Oh, God. Now I had sex on the brain.

Moving towards the bed, Drake gently nudged me so that I was sitting down. He pulled my shoes off, and I watched him kneel at my feet as I ran my fingers through his hair. He reached up to take my coat off and tossed it on his chair. He stared at me as he yanked his own shoes and coat off and dumped them on the floor. He yanked his sweater off, leaving the t-shirt he wore under it on.

"Lie back," he commanded.

I fell backwards, my back resting on the bed while my feet were still on the floor. I felt his fingers pull the snap of my jeans open and slide the zipper down before he tugged them down my legs. He pulled my socks off with them and lightly ran his fingertips upwards, starting at the bottom of my feet. He trailed them up the inside of my legs, pausing as he placed wet, open-mouthed kisses on the underside of my knees. My legs parted, giving him more room. I could feel his hot breath as he slowly moved up my inner thighs. His fingertips had been replaced by his tongue as he moved farther up, his hands holding my legs open for him in a strong grasp.

"I owe you an apology for leaving you to worry so long about Sasha, baby. Think I'm gonna make a new rule for us. Any time one of us needs to make something up to the other, we do it from our knees," he murmured before he ran his tongue around the seam of my panties.

I gasped in response to the rush of moisture his words caused. My panties were drenched and his nostrils flared in response.

"Damn. Think I'm gonna mess up more often if it means I get to taste you each fucking time," he said before yanking my panties down my legs, practically ripping them from my body. "Take your shirt off for me."

I reached down and pulled my shirt over my head. Before I had it all the way off, I felt his lips press against my clit. I couldn't see anything with the shirt covering my eyes, and my other senses felt heightened. I groaned deeply in response to the new feeling.

"You like it when you can't see what I'm about to do. Don't you, baby?"

I looked down at him as I tossed the shirt away. The sight of his wet lips tilted into a smirk drove me crazy. My eyes met his as I nodded my head in response, words failing me as his thumbs rubbed the top of my thighs while he waited for me to respond.

"Don't move. Stay right there," he said as he got up to rummage in his closet.

He came back with a dark red tie in his hand that he placed next to me on the bed.

"Eyes right here," he instructed as he removed his shirt, revealing his sculpted chest. He continued his striptease, slowly popping the button on his jeans and inching the zipper down. My gaze was riveted as I waited for him to pull them down his body. I wanted him naked for me, and he gave me what I wanted as he dropped them to the floor. He stood before me, wearing only a pair of black boxer briefs. His cock strained against them, leaving a dark spot of moisture at the tip. I drank in the gorgeous sight of his body.

"I want to be the last thing you see before I do this," he rasped as he grabbed the tie off the bed and reached to wrap it across my eyes. He knotted it behind my head, leaving me in darkness. "Just feel what I'm doing to your body, Alexa," he whispered into my ear before nibbling his way down my neck.

I felt his fingers pull my bra straps off my shoulders before he lifted me slightly off the bed to undo the clasp at my back. He pulled my bra from my body, and my nipples pebbled even more at the feel of cool air against them. His fingers rolled them gently while he bit my shoulder. I gasped aloud at the contrast of the sting of his teeth and the softness of his hands as he cupped my breasts and licked where he had bitten me.

"Mmmm, I think my Alexa likes when I'm a little bit rough," he whispered into my skin. I felt his fingers move down my body, and he easily slipped one inside of me. "Fuck, baby. You're dripping wet," he groaned.

One thick finger rubbed inside me while his thumb played with my clit. His mouth moved between my breasts, and he alternated between sucking on my nipples and licking around them. Not knowing what he was going to do next was driving me wild. I writhed on the bed, the sheets gripped in my clenched fists while I bit my lip, trying not to scream out.

"Drake, please," I begged.

"Please what, baby? Do you need more?" he asked before plunging another finger inside me. My legs trembled as he pumped two fingers in and out of my body at a painstakingly slow pace. "Or do you need faster?" he teased me before increasing the speed.

My legs tightened around his hand, trying to increase the friction so I could climax. "Yes," I moaned.

"Not yet, Alexa," he chuckled darkly. I felt his other hand grip one of my thighs as he pried my legs apart. "I need a taste of you first."

That was all the warning I got before his lips clamped on to my clit, and it was more than I could take. I reached above my head, wildly searching for a pillow. I found one just in time as I flew over the cliff and screamed into the pillow to muffle the sound.

"So good, baby," Drake muttered as he continued to drive me crazy with his tongue. He pulled his fingers from me and gripped both thighs to keep my legs apart as he licked my sex. I shuddered as aftershocks hit me.

"Drake, oh God. I can't take anymore," I whimpered.

"I don't know. Am I done saying sorry? Do you forgive me yet?" he teased.

"Yes! Totally forgiven."

"You sure?" He tormented me as he sucked my clit back into his mouth and moved his fingers up my thighs.

"What?" I asked, losing track of our conversation at the feel of his fingers sliding inside again.

"Are you sure I'm done? You can't take anymore?" he rasped. He pulled his mouth away and stilled his fingers while they were deep inside me.

"Please," I begged, not even sure what I was asking for anymore.

"Please stop? Or please more? Which one is it, Alexa?" Drake asked.

"More. I need more," I pleaded with him.

"Good, because so do I," he said before pumping his fingers furiously inside me. His tongue teased, circling my clit before moving down to dip inside me as his fingers pulled out. He fucked me with his tongue, hands holding me open as he devoured me. "One more, baby. You can give me one more, can't you?"

I wanted to give him anything he wanted, just so he didn't stop what he was doing. "Yes, one more," I whispered. I reached down and rubbed my clit with two fingers.

"That's right. Help me get you there. I want to watch you come for me, Alexa," he commanded, watching me touch myself. He slid his thumb inside as he lapped at the juices flowing from my body. I tightened around his finger as my body stretched, a second climax rolling over me in waves.

Drake placed a kiss at the top of each of my thighs before moving up my body. He paused to play with my breasts, softly licking each nipple after sucking it into his mouth. A light sheen of sweat covered my body as I lay there panting. I reached up to pull him closer to my body, needing to hold him.

"Damn, baby. Won't ever get enough of that. Watching you come for me has to be the most beautiful thing ever," he whispered into my ear.

I nuzzled into his neck, enjoying our closeness. I still couldn't quite catch my breath, so I just nodded my head. He rolled onto his back and pulled me with him. We lay there together for several minutes, neither of us saying a word. He drew circles on my back, moving from my neck down to the dip in my lower back. Once I had recovered from my climaxes, I kissed a trail up his jaw to his ear.

"Thank you, Drake," I whispered.

"You're welcome, Alexa," he muttered back.

I swirled my tongue in his ear and blew softly. He shuddered in response, goose bumps popping up on his skin. His reaction bolstered my confidence, making me feel powerful. I sat up on my knees and leaned over his body, licking and sucking as I kissed his neck. I ran my hands down his chest, occasionally flexing my fingernails into his skin like a kitten.

"Baby," he hissed in response. "You've got class."

"It's my turn to try out your new rule. I didn't talk to you about how I felt and let everything build up inside instead. How am I going to learn my lesson if I don't pay for my mistake, Drake?"

He used his finger to pull my chin up so he was looking me in the eye. "You don't need to do anything you aren't ready for."

"I am ready for this. I need to show you how much I want you, too."

His eyes flared at my words, and he held my gaze as he nodded. "Fuck, yeah," he muttered.

His eyes stayed locked on me as I moved to kneel between his legs. I leaned over him, my hair brushing across his chest. I could feel the heat of his erection through his underwear as it pressed into my belly. His nipples were hard, and I flicked my tongue over one while rolling the other between my finger and thumb. As I raked my teeth over his nipple, I felt his cock jump in reaction. I moved to the other side and softly blew over his skin before opening my mouth wide and biting down hard. Drake's hips jerked upwards in response, and his hands gripped the back of my head as he held my mouth to him. I sucked hard, leaving a dark red mark behind.

"You like it a little rough, too. Don't you, Drake?" I asked.

He wrapped my hair around one fist before answering. "I like that you wanted to mark me. Trying hard as I can not to pull you up here so I can leave my own mark on your body."

"Maybe later. It's my time to play now," I teased. His hold on my hair tightened a little, letting me know it was my turn because he was letting me have one. I had no doubt that if he wanted to switch roles he wouldn't have a problem convincing me. He let go, and I continued down his body. I savored the taste of his skin, licking and sucking along the way. I swirled my tongue around his belly button and ran my fingernails along the top band of his boxer briefs. He lifted his hips so I could pull them down, and I hiked the fabric up so that I could move them past his jutting erection.

As I worked my way back up his legs, I let my hair trail over his skin. When I reached his cock, I licked the drop of pre-cum from the tip and twirled my tongue around the crown. I sucked the head into my mouth and glanced up to see Drake watching me, his eyes burning with desire. I released him with a popping sound, and he groaned in protest. I slithered up a little and moved so his cock jutted between my breasts. I squeezed them together to increase the friction as I moved up and down. On the downward motion, I stuck my tongue out so I could swirl it around the crown each time it peeked out of the top of my breasts.

Drake's hips pumped in time with my movements, his hands resting on my shoulders. I slowed down on the last stroke, opening my mouth wide and sucking him inside. I heard his breath hiss out, and he fisted my hair tightly.

"Fuck, baby. You're driving me crazy. Suck me deeper," he ordered in a husky tone.

I wrapped a hand around the base and hummed deep in my throat. I twisted my head in one direction and the hand gripping him in the other, rotating back and forth. I felt his erection grow even harder in my mouth. I worked my tongue over his cock, tracing every vein along the way. I wanted to drive him crazy with passion. His hand gripped me harder as his hips jerked up and down in time with my motions. I moved my free hand to his balls and raked my fingernails over them.

"Shit. I'm gonna come," he said as he tried to pull my head away from his body. I tightened my hold on him and shook my head in protest. I sucked him deeper into mouth until I could feel the tip of his cock bump against the back of my throat. I bobbed up and down, quickening my pace. I wanted to send him over the edge, and I got my wish as jets of come exploded from his body in long streams. I swallowed them down as best I could.

His hold on my hair loosened, and I lapped at him with my tongue as I licked drops of semen from his skin. I peeked up at him to find his head thrown back. His eyes were closed and his chest was heaving. I giggled, deliriously happy to have pleased him so much.

His eyes popped open at the sound and he smiled in response. "Changed my mind. Get into as much trouble as you want if that's how you're gonna say you're sorry from now on."

I launched myself into his arms. "Be careful what you wish for. You never know what type of mischief I can find."

"I'm sure I can handle it," he said as he tightened his hold before glancing at the clock. "There's no way you're making it to your other class this morning."

"Don't wanna go, anyway. Just want to stay here with you for a little bit, okay?"

He pulled the blanket up over our naked bodies. "You want me, you got me."

I snuggled into his warmth and my eyes slid shut. I drifted off to sleep and didn't wake up until a couple hours later when my phone buzzed from the pocket of my jeans on the floor. Drake was sleeping soundly beside me, so I reached as quietly as I could to pull my phone out. I had several missed text messages, all from Aubrey asking me where I was and if I was okay. I tapped out a quick response to her, telling her I was with Drake and we were going to miss lunch today. I'm sure she'd have questions for me later.

I dropped the phone back to the floor and cuddled back against Drake. My movements must have woken him up because his arms tightened around me. His stomach growled loudly, making me laugh.

"We missed our normal lunch time at the café," I said.

"Was worth it though," he responded.

"Tell that to your stomach! Sounds like you need food," I teased.

"Worked up an appetite," he said with a smirk on his face. "We can grab lunch downstairs if you want."

"Is that okay?" I asked. I wasn't sure about eating in the frat house. I'd visited Jackson here over the last couple years but hadn't ever eaten with the guys.

"You're with me," he replied, as though that was explanation enough. I guessed nobody would question him about me being there, too.

"Sounds perfect. Then I won't miss my afternoon class, too."

He smacked my butt, but not too hard. "Better get moving if you want to make it in time."

I hopped out of the bed and pulled my clothes back on. I glanced in the mirror and realized my hair was an absolute mess. As I finger-combed it, Drake came up behind me. He was dressed, and he rested his hands on my hips as he watched me in the mirror while I fixed my hair. "Can you make it to my game this weekend?"

I turned in his arms so we were facing each other. "Absolutely. I wouldn't miss it for anything. I'd be a horrible girlfriend if I didn't show up when you're going to win our school a championship."

"Shit, I hope so. That would make my dad a very happy man."

"And you?" I asked.

"I have you. I'm already happy," he said with a sexy smirk.

Chapter 11

WE DIDN'T HAVE far to travel for the American Collegiate Rugby Championship match this year, which was a good thing since Drake's team made it through the single elimination tournament a couple weekends ago and then won our conference title last weekend. It was their first year as an NCAA team, and their success was kind of a shock to everyone. They'd always had a good club team, but they were playing against schools from across the country with really competitive teams this season. I was a little biased, but I couldn't help but think that having Drake transfer here for the team was part of the reason for their unexpected success.

Drake had to travel with the team, so Aubrey and Jackson came with me. We hit the road early Saturday morning to make the four-hour trek to Elkhart, Indiana's Moose Rugby Grounds. Notre Dame's club team was hosting the game. Jackson borrowed an SUV from his dad so we'd have four-wheel drive just in case it snowed again. The bad part about Jackson driving was that he controlled the stereo and wouldn't budge on letting us change the music from his rock 'n' roll to anything else. I was riding in the passenger seat and moved to turn the volume down, but he swatted my hand away.

"Jackson's rules," he reminded.

"No fiddling with the radio," Aubrey and I said in unison, used to his tyranny on road trips.

"You want something, you ask for it," he said.

Aubrey looked up at us with pleading eyes. "Please turn down the music, bro. My head is pounding back here."

"Yeah, Jackson. We're not even asking you to change it. Just turn it down a little. Please," I asked.

"Since you both asked so nicely," he teased as he turned the dial down a few notches.

"Whew! Now we can actually talk without screaming to hear each other!" Aubrey exclaimed, leaning over the console to see us better. "I'm bored back here."

"I'd offer to join you, but I don't think you want to watch me hurl for entertainment," I joked. I didn't do very well on long road trips in the back seat. I usually ended up getting car sick.

"Yeah, I still don't understand how you can fly a frickin' plane without any problems, but if we throw you in the back seat of a car for too long you get sick. There's something wrong with that," Aubrey replied, shuddering a little at the mention of vomit.

I'd only done it a couple times, but any sign of puke made Aubrey sick, too. So we didn't take any more chances after the second time with her chain reaction. I now rode in front any time we were in the car for more than half an hour. I flipped her a sassy grin. "Sucks to be you."

She punched me in the arm. "Don't be a bitch," she complained.

"Enough of that, you two. We're almost there. I'm not going to listen to your whining the rest of the way," Jackson said.

"Wah-wah-wah," I muttered under my breath, earning myself a glare from him. I smiled weakly in return. "Sorry."

Aubrey found it hilarious as she busted up laughing. It took her a few minutes to calm down. "How long is the game?" she asked.

"A couple hours," I answered.

"Ugh! How did you talk me into this again? We'll be in the car longer than we'll actually be there," she complained.

"Hey, you didn't have to come," Jackson reminded his sister. "It's not like you're driving or anything."

"Oh, stop." She glared at her brother. "Like I would miss out on a road trip with my bestie. I'm just cranky."

Luckily, we pulled up at the field a few minutes later, Aubrey pouting a bit in the back seat. "You should have taken a nap on the way," I told her.

"Nah, I'll just grab an energy drink. I'll be fine, and I can sleep all the way back anyway."

We paid to get in, and I saw Drake warming up on the field. He was so sexy in his uniform, sweat already dripping his forehead. As he ran, I watched the pumping of his legs, his thigh muscles clenching as he moved. Jackson waved a hand in front of my face. "Anyone home?"

I looked over at him, startled. "Sorry, I was distracted."

He glanced over at the field to where Drake was and grimaced. "Yeah, I can see that. C'mon, let's grab our seats. It's gonna start soon."

As we sat down, I smiled over at Drake and took off my coat so I could show him my Blythe College Rugby sweatshirt. I turned around so he could see his name on the back and he flashed me a huge grin. I'd taken it to a shop in town so I could surprise him.

"That's gotta make him happy," Jackson muttered when he saw it.

"What?" I asked.

"You've branded yourself as his with his name across your back," he said, tracing his name over the letters.

"Do you really think he likes it?" I asked.

"I'm sure he fucking loves it."

"Yay!" I grinned up at Jackson. "I thought your sister was an idiot for suggesting it. It sounded so high school. But I really wanted to show Drake that I support him today."

"Hey!" Aubrey protested. "You know you should never doubt me like that."

"Sorry," I apologized. "You were totally right. Again."

The match began, and I watched avidly. It was really close, and I couldn't tell if Drake's team was going to manage to pull it off. It seemed like Purdue was going to beat us during the first half of the match. Luckily, I had Jackson with me to explain everything. I was apparently a slow learner when it came to all the rugby slang and rules. A tough series of penalties brought the Boilermakers up 0-12 early on. Blythe had a successful trip into the opposition's try zone, bringing the score to 7-12. I grew worried as Purdue was doing so well. The score remained the same with just a few minutes left in the half.

With a quick turnaround off the restart, we managed to tie the match at the thirty-seven-minute mark. Some quick plays came in the final minutes of the half, seeing a significant attempt to the try zone by Purdue that worked, and a missed conversion brought Purdue ahead by five. With just moments left, Purdue brought in three penalty points by launching the ball through the uprights from thirty-six meters out. The halftime score saw Purdue up 17-25. Things were not looking good for Drake's team.

I watched Drake as the team walked off the field, his head hung low. He was walking stiffly, favoring his right leg. I rushed over to him to make sure he was okay. He waved his teammates ahead when he saw me coming.

"Are you hurt?" I asked worriedly.

He shook his head. "Not really. Just a pulled muscle."

I gave him a quick hug, knowing he needed to get into the locker room with his team. "Hey, you've got this," I reassured him with a kiss on the cheek.

After a short intermission, they came back out looking energized for the next half. Whatever their coach had said to them must have worked because after just five minutes into the second half, we crossed the ball over Purdue's try line, pulling us within one point of the Boilermakers. Maintaining the momentum, Drake's team continued to apply pressure and brought the ball deep within Purdue's half. A successful goal-line stand ended up with a Blythe knock-on, resulting in a Purdue scrum. Luckily, we brought in five more points. The clock kept ticking down, and with a few minutes left in the match, Purdue drew a penalty. They made a penalty kick, bringing the score to within one point. Argh! We couldn't lose this close to the end. Drake would be crushed.

Blythe knew it was now or never, and they really brought up the heat. They had a successful conversion and won the game by eight points. Drake was celebrating with his team on the field, all the guys super excited to have won the championship. He glanced up at me and flashed a wicked grin before charging toward the stands to lift me out of my seat and swing me around.

"We won!" he yelled.

"You were awesome," I breathed into his ear.

"Hell yeah I was. You're my good luck charm, baby," he said.

"How's the leg?"

"What leg?" he joked, letting me know he was fine. He dropped me back onto my feet and swooped down for a kiss. "Can you wait until I get out before you leave? I need to grab a shower."

"Sure. I'm sure Jackson and Aubrey won't mind waiting. It's not like we're in a rush or anything."

"I'll go fast. Just want to see you before I have to get back on the bus."

I watched him walk away before turning back to my friends. "That's okay with you guys, right?"

"Yeah," Jackson grumbled before wandering away.

"Don't mind him," Aubrey said as she bounced down the stands towards me. "He's grumpy today."

Drake had really meant it when he said he'd hurry since he was back in about five minutes. I was talking to Aubrey when he came up from behind and wrapped his arms around me. "Hey, baby. Thanks for waiting."

"Totally worth the wait," I answered as I cuddled into his hold.

"So glad you were here," he said, nuzzling my neck. "It sucks that my parents couldn't make it this weekend. Sent them a quick text to let them know we won, and I'll call them as soon as you head out. Wouldn't have been the same without someone cheering me on today."

"I'm sorry they couldn't come, but at least you'll see them in a couple weeks for Thanksgiving."

"I'm not sure I want to be away from you for that long. Can't you talk to your dad about coming with me? You know my parents would love to have both of you."

"Hey, no fair! No stealing my bestie for the holidays, Drake," Aubrey complained.

"She's my girl, Aubrey. You're lucky I let you steal her from me at all," Drake replied. He gently bit my neck in a possessive gesture that made me squeal in response.

"I'm not sure what Dad would say, but I'll ask," I reassured Drake. "Sorry, Aubrey. A girl's gotta do what a girl's gotta do."

"Yeah, yeah. Just abandon me, why don't ya?" she teased back.

Jackson wandered back over to us and nodded to Drake. "Good game, man."

"Thanks," Drake responded. Several of his teammates headed back our way. "I gotta get back to the team, Alexa. Be safe on the trip back."

"I'll take good care of her for you," Jackson said.

"You better," Drake warned before he turned me around and kissed the heck out of me. He flashed Jackson a triumphant grin before walking away.

"Let's head home," Aubrey said as she dragged me back to the car. "I'm ready for a road trip nap."

The trip back was uneventful since we both fell asleep, leaving Jackson to play his music as loud as he wanted. He dropped us at the dorm, and I headed back inside for more sleep. Drake was going to be back late since the team was going out to eat and celebrate on the way back home. I figured it would be good to catch up on lost sleep as long as I had a night to myself, and I was still tired from the road trip.

Chapter 12

THINGS WERE GOING so well with Drake, and I was excited to make another trip to Connecticut with him. I'd get to fly with my dad and then spend time with Drake over the long holiday weekend. When we went last time, our situation had been so different. I'd felt awkward being around his family since we'd barely known each other, and everyone had assumed we were dating. Now I really was his girlfriend, and I looked forward to getting to know them because they were a huge part of his life.

It would be weird not spending Thanksgiving with Dad and Aubrey's family though. Dad got a last-minute request to do a charter for a past customer whose plans had changed due to an illness in the family, and they were willing to pay a huge bonus because they needed the flight so badly. Dad felt bad for them because it might be the last Thanksgiving their kids could spend with their grandparents, so he felt like he needed to say yes even though it meant missing the holiday with me. I talked it over with Drake and convinced my dad that it was perfect because it meant I could spend the weekend with Drake's family without feeling guilty. Luckily, his charter was on the East Coast, so he could take us to Drake's hometown first before heading up to pick up his passengers.

Aubrey pulled dresses out of both closets and tossed them onto the bed next to my suitcase. "You bitch. I can't believe you are abandoning me on Thanksgiving with my brothers! It's a good thing for you that your boyfriend is super hot, so I understand why you're going with him instead of staying here," she teased. "But you owe me one! And I'm calling in my marker now. Listen up! You absolutely must pack more than you usually do! I know Drake said his parents didn't have anything big planned for the weekend, but you need to be prepared just in case. You got lucky last time being able to borrow this from his sister," she said as she held up the purple dress I had fallen in love with when we were there. I'd brought it home and had it dry cleaned so I could return it to Drea. I figured I'd get the chance to do it in person, so I didn't ship it back to her. I'd left the shoes in the pool house with a thank-you note.

"Well, if you're going to use up your 'I'm abandoning you for Thanksgiving IOU' for this, then I guess I have to listen. What do you think I'll need for four days?"

Aubrey wagged her eyebrows at me in a suggestive way. "Four days and nights, you mean."

"At his family's home! It's not going to be like that."

"That's what you say now, but what do you think is going to happen when Drake gives you that fuck-me look he gets when he's looking at you? Your dad won't be staying with you this time since he has other flights booked, so you'll probably be in the pool house all by yourself. With only Drake to keep you company at night. Go ahead and pack all granny panties. I'm pretty sure you're just going to end up naked anyway. Hell, you could wear a sack and Drake would still want to strip it off and take you hard."

"You are so bad, Aubrey!" I glanced down at the clothes I was packing and pulled out some lingerie to throw into the bag.

"Bad? Who me? You're the one who's listening to my advice. Bring these, too. I bet Mr. Alpha would really enjoy you looking all innocent while he's being naughty," she said as she handed me a matching, white lace bra and panty set.

I smiled, knowing she was right. He really would love the white set. My bag now overflowed with clothes for the weekend. I should be prepared for just about anything planned, but I was still a little nervous. Aubrey made a good point—we'd probably spend the nights together. Away from the house. And I wasn't sure I could survive another night alone with him without us having sex. He had proven to me that he wasn't in this just for the sex by insisting that we wait this long, that's for sure. But I was at the point where I might end up begging!

"Uh-oh, I know that look! Alexa Marie, you're planning something, aren't you?" Aubrey asked in a sing-song voice.

I grinned wickedly at her. "Hmmmm, maybe?"

"Ack! What? Lemme help!"

"I think it's time I make it crystal clear to Drake that I'm ready to take the next step in our relationship. And the lingerie is going to help me send that message."

Aubrey clapped her hands together in excitement! "Yippee! Start with the white set, but add these to it," she said and grabbed an unopened pair of sheer white thigh-highs from a drawer. "Throw these on and there's no way he won't realize that you picked the outfit with his viewing pleasure in mind."

I double-checked everything I had packed with a new goal in mind—to drive Drake wild.

Drake: Ready?
Alexa: Yup, all packed and ready to go! :)
Drake: Be there in 5 minutes.

I headed downstairs to wait for Drake so we would be at the airport on time. Nothing made my dad crankier than late people. He had a full weekend booked, too. He'd squeezed this flight in more for me than anything else. I felt a little guilty that he'd be working all weekend while I would be having fun, but he assured me that I worked hard enough between school and the Mile High flights. He wanted me to take time and enjoy myself, too.

Drake pulled up in his car, and I rolled my bag towards the vehicle so I could put it inside. He hopped out and grabbed it from me. "No way, baby. You don't handle your own bags with me around." I was used to his ways by now and just gave him a quick kiss. "Hop in. We need to get moving."

I got settled into the car and smiled over at Drake when he climbed back inside. "Thanks for picking me up."

"Any time. You looking forward to seeing my family again?"

"Yeah, but I'm a little nervous, too."

Drake reached over and squeezed my hand. "Don't be. They loved you last time and they only spent a couple hours with you at a crowded party. They ask me all the time if I'm treating you right. Especially Drea."

"You're lucky to have her for your little sister. She seemed really sweet, but I can easily picture Drea pestering you about me. She was very excited by the idea of you bringing a girlfriend home."

"Keep that in mind when she pounces on you. She can't wait to see you again. She's threatened to tell you all sorts of embarrassing stories about me growing up, so be prepared," Drake warned.

"Does she have baby pictures to go with these stories? Ones with your naked butt in them?" I joked.

"You don't need photos for that. You can see my ass anytime you want," he offered.

I leveled a flirtatious glance his way. "How about now?" The car swerved to the side of the road as he started to pull over. "No, wait! Save it for later, lover boy. We don't have time right now, but I definitely want a rain check on that offer for tonight."

"Like I said, Alexa. Any time you want."

We arrived at the airport just in time for me to help Dad get everything ready for takeoff. Drake brought our luggage onto the plane and called his parents to let them know when we'd be there. As he talked to them, he waved a hand in my direction and pointed at the doors before he walked outside. We were just finishing up when he strode back inside with an unhappy look on his face. I walked over to him to make sure nothing was wrong with his family.

"Hey, everything okay? Has there been a change in plans on their end?" I asked.

Drake roughly ran his hand through his hair as he pocketed his phone. He gave me a reassuring smile and pulled me into a hug. "Not exactly. Nothing's changed with the weekend in Connecticut, but my mom offered to do a favor for one of her friends. And you're not going to like it."

"Why? If we still get to hang out, then why would it matter to me if your mom is helping a friend?"

"Her friend's daughter wants to come home for the weekend, too. When my mom mentioned that I was taking a charter home, she asked if there was room on board for her daughter to join me."

I pulled away from Drake so I could look him in the eyes. "No, please don't say it was Sasha's mom."

"Yeah, baby, it was. I am so sorry. I had no idea this was going to happen, and my mom is clueless about what a pain in the ass Sasha has been. I didn't want to bother her with it and cause problems between our moms."

I took a step away to pull myself together. Drake knew how much I disliked Sasha because she was always such a bitch to me while she flirted with him right in front of me. I didn't appreciate the bombshell he'd just dropped, but it wasn't like it was his fault. Before I could answer, I heard a car door slam outside and her voice call out for Drake.

"Yay! I'm so excited to go home with you this weekend, Drake," she cooed at him. She turned to look at me, acting like she didn't recognize me. "I have bags in the car that you can put on the plane. Be very careful with them. They're expensive."

"Sasha, cut it out!" Drake snapped at her. "You can get your own bags onto the plane."

"But, Drake. They're so heavy. Besides, having someone to help with things like that is one of the perks of flying privately," she whined.

"Well, it isn't your flight. It's mine and Alexa's. And she doesn't need to help you with anything. You're her guest on the plane. Tell her thank you for letting you tag along and go get your stuff,' he ordered in a hard tone.

"Fine," she huffed. "Your mom mentioned that they booked the flight through her dad. I just figured she was working and was going to let her do her job. But if you're going to be that way, I'll play nice."

She didn't bother with the apology as she stomped back to her car and pulled out four suitcases. I watched her struggle with them and realized that it was going to take forever if she had to get them on board by herself. I nudged him in her direction. "This is ridiculous. Go help her with the bags."

Sasha practically squealed in delight when she realized Drake was helping her. I could hear her chattering on about his muscles as he brought three of the bags over while she rolled one of them beside her. I turned toward my dad, who had joined me, and explained the situation. We needed to update the flight plan since we had an unexpected passenger.

"Want to ride in back with them instead?" he asked as he watched Sasha flirt with Drake.

I shuddered at the thought of being stuck with her for a couple hours. "No way! I've had about as much of Sasha as I can take. Let Drake suffer alone during the flight. It was his mom who invited her along."

My dad chuckled as he walked away from me. I was glad someone was enjoying the situation because I certainly didn't find it amusing. It wasn't a great start to what I had hoped would be a romantic weekend.

I let my dad handle getting our passengers settled for takeoff and just shook my head at Drake when I walked past him. We could talk about it after we'd landed and she wasn't there listening. There was no way in hell I was going to let her know how much she irritated me because it would make her too happy.

I WRAPPED UP everything in the cockpit when we landed, allowing plenty of time for Drake and my dad to help Sasha and her ridiculous amount of luggage off the plane before I got off. My dad was heading farther up the coast to pick up another booking, so I gave him a hug and took some time to chat with him before heading outside.

"Good luck with that one," he said as we were saying our goodbyes.

"I won't need luck, Dad. It's not like I'm spending the weekend with her. I just have to put up with her on the flights. That's all."

"I hope you're right, but I expect she'll do her best to tag along as much as possible," he warned before getting back on the plane.

When I walked outside, Drake was standing next to the limo. Sasha wasn't anywhere in sight, and he must have gotten our luggage into the trunk already. The car doors were closed, and I didn't see the driver either.

"So, that was fun," I said.

He shook his head as he strode towards me. "I hope you mean

that, baby, because I have more bad news. Sasha's riding with us to my parents. Her mom's waiting there to pick her up instead of meeting us here."

"Seriously? Gah, that really sucks. I could ignore her on the plane because I was busy, but now I'm going to be stuck riding in the car with her, too?"

"I wish I could say April Fools or something, but I can't. Promise I will do my best to make this up to you. And I will book a car for her myself if I have to for Sunday."

He wrapped his arms around me as he spoke. From the comfort of his embrace, it didn't sound that bad. It was a relatively short car ride. I just had to survive twenty minutes with her and then I'd have time with Drake.

"I'll add that promise to my rain check to see your ass. I'm sure I'll think of something you can do to make it up to me."

He groaned in my ear. "Fuck, baby. The last thing I want is anyone else in the car with us, let alone Sasha. I was looking forward to all the naughty things I could talk you into doing in the back of a limo."

"It's good to know I won't suffer alone then. You can picture everything I would have let you do to me as we're stuck behaving while she's with us instead."

"Shit, don't torture me like that," he said as he led me back to the limo and helped me inside. He sat next to me and pulled me close to his body, like he was trying to place a wall around me for protection. I relaxed against his warmth and ignored Sasha's chattering the whole way there. She didn't try to draw me into the conversation, and Drake leaned over to kiss the top of my head several times throughout the drive. Each kiss was a reminder that he was talking to her while thinking about me.

The drive to his parents' had seemed so short during the last trip, but it seemed to take forever this time. Sasha just kept flirting with Drake the entire way. It didn't matter to her that he didn't flirt back or that I was practically sitting in his lap. I wasn't sure why, but she didn't seem fazed one little bit by our relationship. I didn't know if I should be irritated or impressed by her persistence. The girl certainly had guts, even though she had no clue that her behavior was more likely to piss Drake off than attract him.

By the time we arrived, I had a raging headache that was most likely caused by the combination of Sasha's perfume and nonstop talking.

Drake got out of the car first and then helped me out. "Gonna be okay?"

I rubbed my temples tiredly and shielded my eyes from the sun. "Not sure. Can you grab my bag first? My migraine medicine is in my makeup bag."

"Sure, baby. Go sit down on the porch, and I'll get you whatever you need. There are some chairs in the shade," he whispered as he pulled his sunglasses off and gently placed them over my eyes.

Sasha had climbed out of the car while we were talking. "Drake, can you help me with my bags?" she asked.

"No, Sasha. I need to take care of Alexa first. You don't even need to do anything with your stuff anyway. The driver will leave them on the steps so they'll be ready to load into your mom's car."

"Oh, but I thought we were all staying here for the weekend. It doesn't look like my mom is here yet. Let me text her to make sure she packed to stay over also."

The pounding in my head increased at the thought of spending even more time in Sasha's company. I raised pain-filled eyes to Drake before turning to walk away. I couldn't deal with her antics right now. I needed to take some medicine and catch a nap. Anything else could wait until I felt better.

As I climbed the steps of the main house, the front door opened and Drea bounced out."Alexa!" she screeched. "Yay! You guys finally made it. I've been waiting forever."

I smiled weakly as I neared her. "Hey, Drea," I greeted Drake's sister.

Drea's smile fell from her face. "Oh, no. You're sick. Here, come sit down."

She helped me over to the chairs and fluffed a cushion behind my back. "You didn't have to come if you weren't feeling well. We would have been disappointed, but we would have understood."

I closed my eyes and leaned my head back. "I'll be fine, Drea. The headache just started. It hasn't had a chance to get really bad."

She looked down to the driveway, where Drake was rifling through my suitcase in search of my cosmetics bag. Sasha stood there, tapping away on her phone, presumably trying to make sure that she got to crash our weekend plans also. "Aha! I get it. Your headache is of the blonde variety. She really can be the biggest pain in the ass. And she's had a crush on Drake ever since we were little. I swear she was about to pee herself when she found out that he was transferring to Blythe."

Even through the pain, I laughed at Drea's comments. "I'm sure she did. She's made it very clear that she's the one who should be dating him and not me."

"Like that's gonna happen. If Drake was the least bit interested in her, it already would have. Besides, I think she's more interested in her mom's fantasies of having her daughter marry her best friend's son than anything else."

"And does your mom have the same dream?" I asked, feeling disheartened by the idea of a pair of matchmaking moms.

"No, my mom's wish would be that Drake finds the right girl to marry. Doesn't matter to Mom where he finds her, just that she makes him happy. Like you seem to do. Now, let me go detach the leech from Drake so he can take care of you. Let me know if you need anything."

Drea made good on her word and kept Sasha busy so Drake could focus on me. He found my Immitrex pills and brought me one along with a tall glass of cold water. He bundled me over to the pool house so I could lie down and take a nap. Before I knew it, I'd slept half the day away and awoke feeling a little better. I tilted my head from side to side to make sure there wasn't too much pain. I felt a rush of relief upon realizing that I'd caught the headache early enough to stop it before it exploded into a full-fledged migraine. Hopefully I'd been fast enough that I'd be back to normal soon.

The house was quiet with no sign of Drake. Our bags were at the top of the stairs, and he had left my cosmetics bag in the upstairs bathroom where I'd easily find it. I brushed my teeth, feeling a bit gross after traveling and sleeping. I was still groggy and pale, so I splashed some cold water on my face. As I dried off with a fluffy white towel, I heard the door close downstairs.

"Drake?" I called.

I heard footsteps on the stairs before he appeared in the bathroom doorway. "Feeling any better?"

"I am, thanks. Sorry I conked out like that."

"No problem. You must have needed the sleep. Hungry?" he asked.

"Yeah, I could eat. Did I miss anything while I was out?"

"Nothing good. My mom invited Sasha and her mom to stay for dinner so I told her we were just going to eat here since you weren't feeling well."

"Was she okay with that? We came here to visit your family. Not hide out together in the pool house."

He crossed his arms over his chest, looking uncomfortable. "She wasn't happy, but she was more worried about how you were doing than anything else. She'll probably stop by to bring over some dinner and check on you soon."

"Look, why don't you just eat dinner with everyone and then bring me back some food later?"

He shook his head in response. "No way, baby. You're my priority here. You don't feel good, and you need me. My mom will get over it. And hopefully she'll take the hint so that Sasha and her mom don't end up staying the whole weekend."

"God, I hope so too. So much for our fun weekend."

Drake walked towards me and stopped inches away. I could feel the heat from his body as he reached up to run his fingers through my hair, gently rubbing my scalp. "You. Me. No school. No work. No practice. Oh, we'll have fun all right, just as soon as you feel up to it. Count on it."

I stepped closer, filling the small amount of space he had left between us. My body molded to his, I relaxed into him and rested my head on his shoulder. "You better deliver on that promise."

He wrapped his arms around me, holding me tightly. "I won't ever make a promise to you that I won't deliver on. You can take that to the bank, baby. Feel up to heading downstairs and resting on the couch? We can watch a movie. I brought some snacks."

"Drake, go have dinner with your family. I'll be fine."

He swept my legs out from under me in a smooth motion and

carried me towards the door. "Already said no. It's nice to see my family, but this weekend was more about time for us than them. I'm not leaving you while you're sick to go have dinner. Drop it, Alexa."

"Put me down. It was just a headache. I'm not really sick, and I'm certainly not an invalid. I can walk downstairs by myself."

"And give up my chance to show you how big and strong I am? Settle down and hold on tight before I drop you," he teased.

I wrapped my arms around his shoulders as he carried me down the stairs. Instead of putting me down once there, he crossed over to the couch and sat down with me on his lap. He reached around me to grab extra pillows and propped my feet onto them. Once he had us settle to his satisfaction, he turned on the television. "Anything you really want to see?"

"Pick whatever you want." I snuggled into his hold, getting comfortable.

Drake turned on an older action movie I had seen before. I enjoyed cuddling with him on the couch and could barely to keep my eyes open as the movie played. About halfway through, there as a knock on the door right before it opened. Drake's mom, Ginny, peeked through the opening and saw us on the couch. "Oh, good. You're awake," she said as she walked inside.

"Hey, Mom," Drake greeted. I wiggled, trying to get free from his hold so I could move away while talking to her. It was awkward to be sprawled on Drake's lap while talking to his mom. His arms tightened around me, making it clear that he didn't want me to move.

His mom saw the struggle and laughed. She lifted a picnic basket up so we could see it. "Don't get up on my account. I just brought over some dinner so you guys don't starve tonight."

"Thank you, Ginny. I'm so sorry I ruined your plans for today," I apologized.

"Don't be silly. You didn't ruin anything. I still got to see my son, didn't I? As long as you guys made it here safe and sound, I'm happy. I just hope your headache is better. Do you need anything for it?"

"No, thanks. I had some medicine with me. I'm feeling much better and should be back to normal tomorrow morning."

Drake piped into the conversation. "Don't worry, Mom. I've got it covered. Alexa has me here taking care of her."

She patted Drake on the head and smiled down at me. "I'm sure you're doing a fine job of it, too. But I'm a mom. That means I can't help but worry over you kids."

His mom was so sweet. She reminded me of Aubrey's mom in many ways. I watched her as she pulled several containers out of the basket and put them in the fridge. "You didn't have to go to so much effort. I would have been fine with sandwiches. I'm usually not that hungry after a bad headache anyway. In fact, I was trying to convince your son to join you all at the house for dinner without me."

Her eyes twinkled in response as she shook her head. "And I'm sure that suggestion went over like a lead balloon. Drake made it very clear earlier that he wasn't excited about having dinner with our guests. He's always been a little uncomfortable around dear Sasha. Your headache gave him the perfect excuse to bow out of tonight. It wouldn't be right for him to leave you alone here feeling unwell while we all had dinner together."

Drake smirked at me. "See, Alexa. My mom says I should stay here, too. Told you so."

She shook her head at him. "Don't give her a hard time, Drake. This is your chance to show her what a great, supportive boyfriend you can be."

I grinned up at him. "Yeah, Drake. Be a good boy and cater to my every whim since I don't feel good."

"And that's different from any other day how?" he teased.

I rested my head on his chest and shrugged my shoulders at his mom. What could I say? He really did treat me well.

"All right, kids. I better get back up to the house and get ready for dinner. Drake, you behave," she said as she wagged her finger at him. "Alexa, get some rest and we'll see you in the morning at breakfast."

She left and I looked up at Drake. "Your mom is pretty awesome."

"Of course she is. She'd have to be for me to be her son, right?" he asked as he flexed his arm, showing off.

"Put those muscles to good use," I said as I pulled his arms around me.

He squeezed me once and started the movie back up. Snuggling with him was so comfortable, and my headaches always wore me out.

The first time I had a migraine, it totally freaked my dad out when I slept for almost two days straight, only getting up to drink something and go to the bathroom. Hopefully I'd caught this one early enough that I wouldn't miss out on Thanksgiving tomorrow. Even with the long nap earlier, I drifted back off to sleep pretty quickly.

WHEN I WOKE up, sunlight was streaming through the windows. I rolled over and realized that Drake had carried me upstairs at some point while I was sleeping. I must have been totally out of it to not wake up while he'd moved me. And apparently while he'd undressed me since I was only wearing one of his shirts and my panties. There was no sign of Drake other than the indentation on the pillow next to me where he must have slept last night.

I spotted my phone on the bedside table and grabbed it. I was surprised to see that it was already after eight in the morning. I'd missed our entire first day here because of that stupid headache. Not exactly the best way to start our trip, but I felt so much better after all that rest.

I hopped out of bed and saw my suitcase in the corner of the room. I opened it and found it empty except for a note inside. I unfolded the note and found Drake's scrawl on it.

Unpacked your stuff. It's in the dresser.
Want to give me something to be thankful for today?
Wear the white!

The last sentence was underlined twice for emphasis. Oh, God! He'd unpacked my bag and found all the lingerie Aubrey had talked me into bringing. Talk about embarrassing. And now my surprise for tonight was ruined. I was pretty sure he'd figured out that I had brought all that stuff for his benefit. Eeek!

I pulled open one of the dresser drawers and found my white panty and bra set at the top of the pile with the matching thigh-highs outside of the package, resting on top. I glanced back at his note and decided to go for it. I might not be able to surprise him anymore, but at least I could drive him wild all day long with him knowing what he'd find under my dress tonight.

I brought my clothes into the bathroom with me and took a quick shower. I was fully recovered from my headache and looking forward to the day ahead. I felt incredibly sexy as I put on my clothes and couldn't wait to torture Drake since he'd know right away that I'd followed his instructions.

I headed downstairs and found Drake fixing coffee in the kitchen. I snuck up behind him on tiptoes and placed my hands over his eyes.

"Guess who?" I whispered into his ear.

"My hot-as-shit girlfriend?" he answered before he turned and lifted my hands off his face. Grabbing my hips, he moved me back a little to rake his gaze down my body. His eyes burned when they rested on my stocking-clad legs. He reached a finger out and ran it up my thigh, lifting the bottom of my dress until he reached the top of the stockings. He whistled under his breath.

"Wouldn't want you to not be thankful today of all days," I teased.

He let the fabric drop back down and looked into my eyes. "I already was 'cause you're with me, but you just gave me something to look forward to for later, baby. Surprised the shit out of me when I saw what you'd packed for this trip."

I blushed and looked down at the floor. "I'm sure it did," I muttered.

Drake pulled my chin up and forced me to look at him. "Best surprise ever. Feel free to shock the hell out of me as often as you want with shit like that."

I wrapped my arms around his neck and whispered into his ear. "I was hoping my choice would help convince you that I'm ready. I don't want to wait anymore, Drake. I need you."

"Damn," he groaned at my words. "I wish we didn't have to meet everyone for breakfast so I could show you how much I want you. Tonight. Don't think I could hold out any longer."

"Thank you for making me wait," I whispered. "I didn't get it at first, but I do now. And I'm glad we held out because it will mean more now that we know each other so well."

"Still would have meant a lot if we'd fucked before, baby. But I needed to make sure you were completely ready to be mine before I had you. There's no way in hell I'm letting you go after tonight."

I shivered at his possessive tone. "I'm not going anywhere, Drake. I'm yours already."

He smacked my butt before kissing the top of my head. "Damn straight you are."

Drake picked me up and put me on the island countertop. He poured me a cup of coffee, adding creamer and sugar so it was exactly the way I liked it. I took a sip and my stomach growled loudly.

"You skipped too many meals yesterday. I should have woken you up and made you eat something last night," he said as he grabbed a banana and handed it to me. "Eat this."

"No, I'm glad you didn't wake me. I needed the sleep more than food, Drake." I unpeeled the banana and wrapped my lips around the tip. Once I knew I had his full attention on my mouth, I took a big bite and grinned at him.

"Ouch! You better watch those teeth later." He shuddered, pretending to be scared. I chomped on the banana again, exaggerating the action for emphasis. "C'mom, let's go find you some real food."

He pulled me off the counter and handed me my coffee mug. I quickly finished the banana and threw the peel into the garbage so we could head up to the house to spend the day with his family.

Chapter 13

THANKSGIVING WITH DRAKE'S family was a riot. Drea was no help at all in the kitchen, so I hung out with his mom while Drake watched football with his dad. We cooked a huge feast, and I figured they'd have tons of leftovers. I hadn't counted on how much of an appetite Drake and his dad would have. They devoured the meal and disappeared for even more football on TV. Drea helped with cleanup, and it was time for Drake and me to head back to the pool house before I knew it.

"Thanks for dinner, Mom," he said as he walked into the kitchen.

"You're welcome, but you better thank your girlfriend too. It was nice having someone around who was interested in helping me cook," she answered.

"Mom," Drea squealed in protest.

"Drea, I love you more than anything, my darling daughter, but you know your talents don't extend to the kitchen," their mom teased.

"At least I helped clean up the mess. That's more than Drake can say he did," she taunted her brother.

"This is true," I agreed. "Did you bring me with you just so I could cook and clean for you?"

Everyone laughed, and Drake pulled me close. "I'll show you why you're here as soon as we're alone," he whispered into my ear.

"You guys go on now. We're almost done in here," his mom offered.

Drake grabbed my hand and pulled me to the door. "You don't

have to tell us twice. See you guys later," he threw over his shoulder as he practically dragged me out.

"Hey, slow down," I protested, stumbling behind him.

"No time for that," he said as he picked me up. He tossed me over his shoulder and patted my butt.

"Drake, put me down!" I howled in protest, laughing at his antics.

"Hell no! I've got plans that can't wait," he replied as he rushed to the pool house. He threw the door open and turned to flip the lock. "Plans that don't involve anyone interrupting us."

He rushed up the stairs. His long strides had me bouncing on his shoulder, laughing. I kicked off my shoes, and he pounced on me. His body pressed mine into the mattress, and I wrapped my arms around him. Drake sat up and pulled his shirt off, tossing it onto the floor. He reached down, slid the bottom of my dress up, and exposed the thigh-high stockings to his gaze.

"So fucking sexy. You drove me crazy today, knowing what was waiting for me under this dress," he rasped as his finger moved up toward my panties and felt how damp they were.

"I drove myself crazy, too," I admitted.

"I can tell," he said before he ripped them from my body. Drake pulled me to a sitting position and lifted my dress over my head. He flicked open the fastener of my bra and tossed it over his shoulder before cupping my breasts in his hands.

"Please, Drake," I gasped as I arched my back toward him, pressing my breasts farther into his hands.

He bent his head to the first one, plucking at the hardened peak with his lips. He grazed it with his teeth and licked softly to soothe the sting, drawing moans from me. When he switched to the other side, I moaned. I reached down to hold his head to my body, but he pushed my hands away.

"No, Alexa," he said with a smirk. He moved my hands over my head and pinned them by the wrists. "I'm in charge. Keep your hands up here for now."

I squirmed against him, desperately wanting to get closer and nodded my head.

"Such a good girl. You deserve a reward."

He gripped my hands and pulled me off the bed until I was on my knees on the floor. I unzipped his pants and sucked his cock into my mouth as he thrust inside. He stroked my face with one hand as he used the other to guide my head. I was happy to give him control, not thinking while I just enjoyed the pleasure I was feeling as he had his way with me.

"Enough, baby," he rasped out as he urged me to stand again before he pushed me down onto the bed. "Don't move," he ordered. I could hear the rustle of his pants as he kicked them off, now standing gloriously naked before me. He pushed my legs open.

"I need to hear you come before I fuck you for the first time," he growled. His raspy tone drove me even wilder. His hands gripped my thighs, right where the top of the stockings reached. His lips wrapped around my clit, and I exploded without warning. The climax surprised me, and Drake prolonged it with flicks of his tongue and light sucks.

I could barely catch my breath. "Take me now," I rasped out.

He pressed the head of his erection against my wetness. He felt so big against me, and I couldn't wait to feel him inside.

"Are you on the pill?" he asked as he eased the tip inside.

"Yes," I whispered, wiggling my hips.

"I've never fucked without a condom before, baby. Haven't been with anyone else in months, and my physical showed that I was clean. I wanna go bareback with you."

I nodded my head at his request and threw my legs around him as he plunged inside. He held still, deep inside. It felt amazing to have him hard and hot within me.

"You feel so damn good," he groaned.

I lifted my hips, trying to move him even deeper. "Drake," I moaned.

"Beg me, baby. I promise to make it good for you, but I want to hear you beg."

His dominant tone made me drip with need. "Please, Drake. I need you."

He bent his head to nibble on my nipple, biting down hard enough to leave a mark. "Alexa, you can do better than that. How do you need me? What do you want me to do?"

"Please, fuck me. Drake, I need you to move," I begged.

"Much better," he rasped before he pulled out and plunged back in on a hard stroke. I moved my hands from where he'd put them above my head and held on as he picked up speed. I raked my nails down his back as he moved harder inside me. I closed my eyes as waves of pleasure rolled over my body. Drake stopped moving, staying lodged deep inside my sex.

"Open your eyes, baby. You know I want to see you come for me," he commanded. I slowly opened them and found him staring at me with a passion-filled stare. "That's right. Show me how good I make you feel."

"Oh, God. Don't stop. I'm so close," I begged, my body quivering with need. He started to move again, slowly stroking in and out of my body. I needed him to move harder to push me over the edge. My hips slammed up to meet his thrusts, and I dug my nails into his ass as I tried to spur him on. He paused on an upward thrust and grabbed my hips in a controlling grip.

"Hold on, baby. Trust me to get you there."

I relaxed my grip and he started to move again, harder now as he hammered into me. I clenched around him, and my legs started to shake as I hung suspended on the edge. Drake leaned down and nibbled his way up my neck to my ear.

"Come for me now," he whispered, licking inside my ear as his finger found my clit. The combination sent me over, and I convulsed around him. He gentled his strokes, lengthening my orgasm for what felt like hours. When it ended, he rolled onto his back with me on top. "Ride me."

I swiveled my hips, thrilled to watch Drake's face as I moved over him. I wanted to give him as much pleasure as he had just given me. I leaned down and bit gently on his lower lip before kissing him deeply. His hands gripped my hips as he started to thrust upwards. I could feel him start to swell inside me.

"Come inside me, Drake," I whispered.

My words triggered his climax, and Drake cried out as his body stiffened when his own orgasm washed through him. His cock throbbed deep inside me, semen jetting in streams into my body. I collapsed on top of him, completely drained of energy.

When he recovered, he pulled me into his arms and rolled to the side. "Fuck, baby. That was even better than I thought it would be. You okay?" he asked.

"Yeah, I'm fantastic," I said with a smile, curling up against him. I took a deep breath, inhaling his scent deep into my lungs. I'd never felt anything this good before in my life. It scared me a little how he made me feel. I snuggled closer, pulling his arms around my waist.

"This feels good," he said, kissing the back of my neck. We drifted off to sleep spooned together.

We spent the rest of the weekend at the pool house, only joining his family for dinner. We made love several more times and snuggled in front of the TV, watching holiday movies. The days together were perfect, drawing us closer together. When time came for us to leave on Sunday, I was sad to go. I knew that our time together on campus wouldn't be the same.

THE WEEKS AFTER Thanksgiving flew by. We spent as much time as possible together, and I slept at Drake's room in the frat house most nights. His schedule had opened up quite a bit since the Rugby team's winter season was over for College 7s. He had a little break before the spring season would start after the holiday break.

And the sex—it was amazing. We couldn't seem to get enough of each other. I'd never really thought of myself as an overly sexual person, but with Drake, everything was different. He just had to turn his dark gaze my way and it would turn me on. He enjoyed teasing me throughout the day with little touches whenever we were together. By the time night rolled around, I was usually so turned on that I was ready to jump his bones.

I'd even slowly started to leave more items at his place so I didn't have to do the walk of shame in the mornings if I forgot to pack a change of clothes before he picked me up.

Since the weather had gotten bad, Drake didn't like for me to drive to the airport by myself when I had a charter booked. He thought the Mini wasn't very safe in the snow. So he drove me and studied in Dad's office until I was ready to leave.

Things hadn't gone as expected for the couple I'd taken up based on the death glares the wife was sending her husband when I let them know they needed to buckle up for landing. He looked pretty happy with himself, so I can only guess that he was a little too excited by his foray into the Mile High Club. Between the tension her frustration caused and the storm front coming our way, I was very happy that Drake was waiting for me.

I wrapped everything up with the couple and got the plane situated as quickly I possibly could. By the time I made it into the office to grab Drake, I was so hungry that my stomach was growling loudly.

"Feed me! I'm hungry!" I cried as I bounded into the room.

He tossed me a Milky Way from his stash on the desk. "Can't have my baby go hungry. This should tide you over 'til we can grab some dinner."

"Yay! My favorite," I squealed.

"I know. Why do you think I eat them now?" he asked.

"You are the sweetest, bestest boyfriend in the whole wide world," I whispered as I kissed him quickly on the lips before chomping on my candy.

"And don't you forget it," he threatened with a mock stern glare.

We headed for his car, and a light snow was starting to fall. It was a gorgeous sight, but it was very cold outside. "Brrr," I shivered as I buckled up.

Drake turned up the heat and tossed a blanket from the back over me. "How did you ever survive Midwestern winters without me?"

"No clue. I really should move to California or Hawaii or somewhere like that. The snow is beautiful, but I miss the warmth and the sun!" I teased.

"Maybe we can come up with a compromise when we graduate," he answered, stunning me since he was basically saying we'd be together a year and a half from now.

"Maybe," I whispered, smiling at him.

We went through a drive-thru for food and settled on Drake's bed to eat. I would have laughed if someone had told me that eating French fries could be sexy, but that was before Drake. Pretty much anything he did was hot. He finished his food before me, so I fed him some of my fries. He nibbled on my fingertips with each bite, licking off any salt that remained. I hurried through my meal, wanting him more than food even though I'd been starving only minutes before.

I gathered up our trash and moved to the bed to straddle his lap. My nipples puckered as he watched me from hooded eyes. I had just lowered myself onto his lap when my phone chimed. I pulled it from my back packet to put it on the bedside table and realized that I had several missed texts from Aubrey.

"Hold on a second. Something's up with Aubrey," I said as Drake lowered my shirt to kiss the tops of my breasts.

"Grrrr," he growled as he nuzzled my chest.

Aubrey: Sleep here tonight?
Aubrey: Need to talk.
Aubrey: Are you coming?

As badly as I wanted Drake right now, I couldn't abandon my best friend if she needed me, and it sounded like she did. She wouldn't have asked me to come back if she didn't.

"Shit," I swore. "I need to head back to my dorm."

Drake pulled his head away to look up at me with a frustrated glare. "Fuck. Gimme five minutes."

I leaned down and gave him a deep, wet kiss before pulling away to stand up. "No can do, dude. It's gotta be bad for her to send me three texts in a row. Hold on to that thought though. You know I'll see you tomorrow. And if it isn't too horrible, maybe I'll be able to come back later."

"Fine," he huffed with an adorable pout on his full lips.

I grabbed my stuff and we headed over to the dorm.

"I'll text you once I know what's going on, okay?" I said when we got close to my building.

"Let me know if she needs anything. I'll run out and grab it for you. No driving your damn car in the snow!"

"Yeah, yeah, yeah. Talk to you later," I said as I left the car.

When I got to our suite, I found Natalie and Faith waiting for me in the common area. Faith jumped up as I walked in the door and shoved a box of tissues at me.

"Thank God you're here. She's a total mess," she said. "She stormed in about an hour ago and locked herself in your room."

"She hasn't come out at all?" I asked, glancing at the closed door.

"No, and we haven't heard anything other than crying, either," Natalie answered. "I knocked and asked her if she was okay, but she just screamed at me to go away."

"She's been acting kind of strange lately, too. You've been pretty busy with Drake, so you might not have noticed. But I don't think she's been sleeping very well. I've found her in here a few times when I've woken up to go to the bathroom," Faith added.

"Crap. That doesn't sound good at all. Thanks for waiting to tell me what's going on," I told them as I headed towards our door.

"We like Aubrey. We were about to head out, but we didn't want to leave her until you got here," Natalie said.

"Yeah, I hope it isn't anything serious," Faith chimed in.

"Me too," I muttered under my breath, knowing that it was very unusual for Aubrey to freak out like this. I knocked on the door lightly. "Aubrey, it's me. Will you let me in?"

I heard her rush to the door right before it swung open. "Finally!" she shrieked as she pulled me into our room.

"What the hell's going on, Aubrey?" I asked.

She turned towards me, and I gasped when I saw her face. She was always so put together, but her hair was a mess and mascara was streaked down her cheeks. She really had been crying this whole time.

"I'm scared, Lex," she whispered.

I walked over to her and pulled her into a hug. "Why? Did someone hurt you?"

"I think I might be pregnant," she cried, shaking in my arms.

"What?" I gasped.

"I'm late. You know I'm never late—like ever."

"How late?" I asked.

"Almost a week."

I pulled away to look into her face. "Aubrey, why didn't you tell me?"

She shrugged her shoulders and looked down at the floor. "I think I was trying to pretend it wasn't happening. Lex, what will I do if I'm pregnant? I can't get an abortion, and I'm so not ready to be a mom. My parents are going to kill me."

"If you're pregnant, we'll figure it out. Your parents might not be happy, but you know they'll support you. They would never let you go through something like this alone. They love you," I reminded her.

"I know that, I do. But I just don't know how I can tell them what's going on."

"Have you taken a test yet?"

She shook her head in response. "No. I bought a couple today, but it says they work best first thing in the morning."

I pulled out my phone and Googled pregnancy tests to get more information. "Okay, it says here that you can still take one now, it's just less accurate. I think you should do that, and if it's positive then you'll know and that part will be over. If it's negative, then you can take the other one in the morning. Okay?"

"Yeah, but can you check if Faith and Natalie are still here? I feel weird doing this with them hanging around."

"I think they're gone, but I'll double-check," I assured her. I went into the common area, and there was no sign of either girl. "The coast is clear."

I waited outside the door as Aubrey used the bathroom. When I heard the toilet flush and running water, I opened the door to check to make sure she was okay. The pregnancy test was sitting on the corner of the counter, like a ticking time bomb.

"We have to wait a few more minutes," she said before she slid down and sat on the floor.

I crouched in front of her. "Do you need anything?"

"I could really use a shot of vodka right about now, but I guess that's not an option," she complained.

"Not tonight, but we can drink ourselves silly tomorrow night if the tests both come back negative," I promised.

"I'm so glad you came back. I'm sorry to interrupt your time with Drake tonight."

"Shut up! Where else would I be when my best friend is having a crisis? I'm right where I need to be, and we could have done this sooner if you'd just have told me about it," I chastised her. "What pushed you over the edge tonight?"

"The guy I was with last, the one who could be my baby daddy? I saw him today. It's been a few weeks, and I'm the one who said no to a relationship. But I freaked out when I saw him with another girl, and here I am, worried that I might be pregnant with his baby. It just made it seem more real."

"Aubrey," I sighed.

"Here goes nothing," she muttered as she got to her feet and lifted up the test to check the results. "Thank God! It's a minus sign."

I jumped up and hugged her. "One down, one to go. Let's get you some water so you'll have to pee in the morning. We can wake up early and take the next one, okay?"

She sighed deeply and nodded her head. I sent Drake a quick message, letting him know that I wouldn't make it back over. Aubrey and I chatted into the night, catching up on everything that had been going on with each other. I felt guilty talking about how well things were going with Drake and me when her life was so messed up right now. Aubrey had always flitted from one boy to the next, falling in and out of love so easily that she never really bruised her heart. I'd always kind of admired her for it, actually. Now, I realized that she hadn't really been falling in love. Infatuation? Sure. Lust? Probably. Love? No way.

I hadn't thought of my feelings for Drake in those terms before, but I had to admit that I'd fallen for him. Hard. I couldn't imagine my life without him in it. My days were better when we were together, and he made my heart race every time I saw him. As I finally drifted off to sleep, I had to admit it, at least to myself. I had fallen hopelessly in love with Drake Bennett.

A few short hours later, I woke to the blaring of my alarm. It was only 5:00 a.m., but we'd figured it was late enough for the second pregnancy test. I shook Aubrey awake and led her to the bathroom. I waited while she peed on it, and we repeated the process from the night before, whispering to each other this time so we didn't wake up Faith or Natalie. The last thing we needed right now was any questions about what we were doing.

"I think it's time," I said after five minutes.

"I can't look," Aubrey cried. "You do it this time."

I got up and checked the test. I turned to her, beaming. "Negative. It's a minus sign, Aubrey."

"I'm not pregnant?" she gasped.

"Nope, you're not. I know you've always been super regular, but maybe it was just stress. Or your body is trying to sync up with ours since there are four of us rooming together."

"I'm not pregnant," she repeated, tears streaking down her cheeks.

I wrapped her up in a hug. "Vodka for sure," I whispered into her ear and she giggled.

"Absofuckinglutely!" she agreed. "But first I need some more sleep so I can face classes today."

"Great idea!" I agreed, and we both headed back to bed.

Chapter 14

I WOKE UP TO the text message chime on my phone. I glanced at the clock and realized only a couple hours had passed. It was barely after 7:00 in the morning.

> **Drake: Meet me asap. Need to talk NOW!**
> **Alexa: What's up? Sounds like an emergency. Not sure I can deal with another one today.**
> **Drake: Meet me at my place asap.**
> **Alexa: You're scaring me. R u ok?**
> **Drake: Not ok. Need to talk.**
> **Alexa: On my way now. Be there in 5 mins.**

Drake's text messages freaked the hell out of me. His tone was different than usual, and he sounded pissed off. I couldn't imagine what had changed since I'd seen him last night. I changed out of my pajamas as quickly as possible and raced over to the frat house. I could hear the loud music that was blaring all the way from the bottom of the stairs. Not a good sign.

As I neared Drake's door, the lyrics from Limp Bizkit's *My Way* got even louder. I went into his room and found Drake sitting on the bed with his head in his hands. I turned the music off and walked over to him. He was staring at me with a blank look on his face, none of the usual twinkle or desire in his eyes.

Kneeling on the floor at his feet, I reached out to rest my hands on his legs. He flinched away from my touch and stood. Striding across the room, he slammed the door shut. I jumped at the sound. I might not know what had happened between now and last night, but it was clear that Drake was angry. I couldn't have even done anything—I'd fallen asleep as soon as I'd texted him last night.

"Drake, what's wrong?" I asked, worried by his silence.

Drake glared at me and crossed his arms over his chest. It was like he was putting up a wall between us. "I need you to tell me how you're paying for school."

"What do you mean how I'm paying for school? The usual way that people pay for college. I have a scholarship, loans, and my job with Dad. Why?"

"And that's it? Because that's not what I heard this morning," Drake responded.

"You heard something about me and school this morning? You haven't even left your room yet." What could someone have possibly said to him that would have gotten him this angry at me?

"Is there a reason that people would think that you're prostituting yourself to pay for school, Alexa?"

"What? Absolutely not! How could you even ask me a question like that?" I was horrified. Here I was, the morning after I'd finally admitted to myself that I had fallen in love with Drake, and he was asking me if I was a hooker.

"I need you to be completely honest with me. I heard from a very good source that something isn't right with your financial situation and that you've resorted to selling sex to pay for school."

"Drake, I haven't even had sex with anyone other than you in like three years. Listen to what you are asking me. You know that's just not possible."

"You said it had been that long, but how do I know if you told me the truth? This information had to come from something you're doing. Please, tell me there's a good explanation, babe. Because I'm about to lose my shit thinking about you with other guys for money. Jesus, for any reason. What the fuck, Alexa?"

"You really believe this crap, Drake? You're honestly asking me if I'm a frickin' hooker? Is that what's happening here right now?" My mind was blown. I couldn't think straight. My heart was racing in my chest. This felt worse than when I'd found out Brad had cheated on me. Even worse than when I was scared to death when he wouldn't leave me alone after we'd broken up.

He ran is hands through his hair in frustration. "I don't want to believe it, babe. I just need you to explain to me why—"

I didn't let him finish his thought as my temper flared. "You know what? No! You don't just need anything from me. I don't owe you any explanations about how I pay for school or what's going on with my dad's finances. This isn't cool, Drake. You know me—or at least I thought you did. I can't believe you would listen to someone say crap like this about me without beating the shit out of them, let alone decide to question my honesty and morals. What the hell?"

He looked shocked at my response, like I didn't have the right to be angry here. "You don't understand. The person who called me about this—"

I held up my hand, stopping him from saying anything more. "I'm not the one here who doesn't understand. You are. I don't care who the person was. You're my boyfriend. You won't even let other guys look at me without getting pissed. Anyone flirts with me and you get all growly and possessive. But someone tells you that I sleep with people for money to pay for school and your first thought is to order me over here by text to accuse me of prostituting myself?"

"Alexa, fuck. What the hell am I supposed to do here, not ask you about this?"

"But you didn't just ask me! You actually believe this crap. God, I really know how to choose guys to fall for," I cried out as I moved towards the door.

"I didn't say that I believed it. I'm asking you to explain to me why someone would think this is what you're doing."

"Well, don't worry about it anymore because it's officially none of your damn business. We're over!"

I stormed out of his room and ran down the steps. My heart was shattered into a million pieces. Tears streamed down my cheeks as I struggled to hold everything inside until I made it back to the safety of my dorm room. Each step I took felt like another nail in the coffin to my relationship with Drake. I ran as fast as I could, hoping that Aubrey was still in our room.

I heard Drake call my name as he chased after me. I couldn't deal with him right now. If he really loved me, how could he possibly believe anything so horrible about me? I moved faster, desperate to get away. As I reached the front door and flung it open, I ran straight into Jackson. His arms reached out to steady me.

"Lex, what's wrong? Did someone hurt you? Tell me you're okay," he demanded.

"Jackson, please. Let me go. I need to leave. Now."

He glanced up and saw Drake coming towards us. "What the fuck? Did Drake do something to you?"

"I can't. Please, I am begging you. I can't be here right now." My voice shook as I lost the battle against the pain that was consuming me.

Drake reached us and went to grab my arm to pull me towards him. Jackson stepped between us, shoving me behind the safety of his body. "Stop right there, Drake. I don't know what the fuck happened, but you're scaring Alexa."

"You're right, Jackson. You don't know what the fuck happened and this has nothing to do with you. Back the fuck off and let me talk to my girlfriend. She has some fucking explaining to do."

I sobbed at the anger in his tone and clutched the back of Jackson's shirt. "Not your girlfriend, Drake."

Drake growled in frustration. "My damn girlfriend!"

"Not what she says, man. Don't know what you did to fuck this up so badly, but you're not doing this with her now. The only way you're getting to her is if you go through me. Walk away now."

"You'd like that, wouldn't you? Your chance to be the big hero. Have you had a taste of her too, Jackson?"

"Jesus, what the fuck are you saying? Shut the hell up before you say something you'll regret forever. Out of all the guys in the world, she picked you. And you're going to fuck it all up over some bullshit like that? You deserve to lose her." He shoved Drake backwards and turned to nudge me out the door. He slammed it shut behind me, giving me time to get away and staying behind so that Drake couldn't chase after me anymore.

I sent a quick text to Aubrey asking her to meet me at her car and to bring a couple changes of clothes for me. My hands shook as I waited for reply, hoping she wasn't still sleeping. My phone chimed moments after I hit the send button.

Aubrey: On my way.

God, that was part of why I loved her like a sister. When the shit hit the fan, she didn't waste any time with unnecessary questions. She took care of business and saved the talk for later, even when she must have been feeling like shit after the drama from last night.

By the time I made it to her car, she was already there. She took one look at me and ushered me into the car. She grabbed a package of tissues from her glove compartment and tossed them into my lap. I collapsed, sobs racking my body now that I was safe in her car.

She tore out of the parking lot, getting me off campus as quickly as she could. Aubrey drove aimlessly, waiting for me to calm down. After about thirty minutes, she pulled over in front of a Holiday Inn on the outskirts of town. "Back in a second. Don't move."

I wasn't sure how long she was gone, but she opened the door and unbuckled my seatbelt when she returned. As I climbed out of the car, she pulled a bag from the back seat. "C'mon, I got us a room."

I followed her blindly, tears obscuring my vision. She held on to my hand as she led me through the hotel lobby and upstairs to a room with double beds. I flung myself onto the closest one, and Aubrey sat next to me and whispered soothing words while she rubbed my back. Once the sobs subsided, she wiped my face with a wet washcloth and brought me a glass of water with a couple ibuprofen. My head was pounding, and I sipped just enough water to swallow the pills down.

"What happened, Lex?"

"I'm not sure, Aubrey. I got a text from Drake that he needed me to come over. When I got there, the things he said… I just don't know what happened. How could he think those things about me?" I looked at her, my eyes begging her to make me understand.

"What things, sweetie?"

"He called me a whore! He actually thinks that I take money from men for sex. I let him in my life, in my fucking body. And he thinks I'm worse than a slut."

"What? You've got to be kidding. That's fucked up, Lex."

I barked out a laugh, nothing humorous in my tone at all. "I wish I were kidding. God! I have the worst taste in men in the history of the world. What the hell is wrong with me, Aubrey? First I pick a cheater who stalked me and now a guy who's willing to believe that I'm a hooker. That I'm turning tricks to pay for college of all things."

"Why on earth would he think that's how you're paying for school? He knows you fly with your dad."

"He said something about my dad's finances. By then I wasn't really listening. I couldn't really focus on what he was saying."

"We'll figure this out, Lex. I'm sure it was just all one big misunderstanding."

I shook my head. "No, there's nothing to figure out. I broke up with him and left. Drake chased after me and Jackson stopped him so I could leave. It's over. I'm done."

Aubrey wrapped her arms around me. "Don't say that. You love him. Are you ready to walk away completely, not even knowing what made him say what he did?"

"Aubrey! How could I ever trust him again after he made an accusation like that?"

"I'm not saying you need to forgive him, but maybe you should at least hear him out once you've calmed down. Maybe you're right and it's better that you end it. But what if you're wrong? What if there's an explanation of some kind? Can you handle ending things with him and seeing him on campus? Seeing him with other girls?"

The thought of him with someone else made me want to vomit. "I…I don't know. I can't imagine any explanation that would be good enough for me to forgive this. I told him he was only my second lover. That means he thinks that I'm a liar, too."

"Take some time for yourself. Think about what you want to do. If you decide to walk away, you have my support. And if you want to talk to him to get to the bottom of all this, I'll respect that, too. You're the only one who knows what the right decision is here. No matter what, you've got me in your corner. Pinky swear." She held her pinky out for me to shake. Even at the height of my despair, the gesture made me smile, remembering all of the promises from our childhood.

"Love you, Aubrey. Thanks for coming to my rescue."

"Shut up, Lex. You gave me the lecture last night when I thanked you for being there for me. You know that's what best friends are for. Now, I rented the room for the whole weekend. The jerk at check-in even made me pay for last night so I could get into the room now instead of waiting until this afternoon."

"Asshole," I muttered, mad at men in general right now.

"How about we hang out, eat junk food, and watch movies all weekend?"

"Don't forget about our plans involving vodka," I reminder her.

"Yes, and vodka. Why don't you send your dad a text letting him know you and I are having a girls' weekend? I'll let my 'rents and Jackson know, too. We'll turn the phones off and pretend that the outside world doesn't exist for a couple days. No pressure to make a decision until you're ready. It will be good for me too after how freaked out I've been this past week."

"Yes! That sounds like exactly what I need to do." I opened my phone and noticed that I had several missed calls from Drake and Jackson, along with a dozen text messages. I resisted the temptation to open any of them and typed out a quick message to my dad. He was out of town on a charter, so he wouldn't expect to hear from me that much anyway. "Can you let your brother know I'm okay when you send your message? He's already tried calling me."

"Already done. Didn't give a lot of details to Mom and Dad, but I did let Jackson know that you were safe with me and that I had everything under control. Now, off with the phones!"

We powered down our phones and Aubrey tossed them into the bag she brought with us. "What did you pack?"

She pulled my favorite pair of pajamas out and handed them to me. "Figured we'd need comfy clothes. So I brought jammies and yoga outfits. It sounded like an emergency, so I didn't bother with much else. And we'll have to order in food 'cause I'm only going out once for supplies since I skipped packing my makeup."

"Wow! You left home without makeup knowing that you might not come back tonight? You really do love me!" I joked, distracted by the idea of my fashion-plate bestie hanging out all weekend with me in casual clothes and no makeup, especially since her eyes were still puffy from crying last night.

"I do, Alexa. And I don't know what happened with Drake, but

I would have sworn that he loves you too," she said in a gentle tone. "We don't have to talk about it now. We can cuddle in bed and watch chick flicks and cry all weekend. Nobody knows where we are right now, so you don't need to think about it yet. Now go change into your jammies and wash your face. I'll pull up the movies and make the first pick, okay?"

I nodded, trying to stem back more tears. I flipped on the light in the bathroom and shut the door behind me. As I turned towards the sink, I caught sight of my reflection in the mirror. I was a total mess with my hair all over the place, pale skin, and dark smudges under red-rimmed eyes. How I felt inside was even worse. My hands were shaking and my stomach was turning. My mouth felt like I had swallowed a bunch of cotton, so I poured myself a glass of water. I gulped a little down and my stomach rolled in protest.

I sank to my knees and crawled to the toilet, glad that I hadn't eaten any breakfast this morning. I spat the water into the bowl and prayed that I wouldn't start to dry heave. I sat there on the floor, trembling for a few minutes until Aubrey knocked on the door.

"Did you fall in or something?" she asked.

"Or something," I answered weakly. "I'll be out in a minute."

After flushing the toilet, I stood on shaky legs and changed into the pajamas Aubrey had brought for me. I opened the door and found her sitting cross-legged right outside waiting for me.

She jumped up and pulled me into a tight hug. "I'm so sorry I can't make it all better for you, Lex. I really wish I could fix this."

I gave her a quick squeeze before pulling away. "You're helping, Aubrey. I don't know what I would've done today without you. I don't know that anyone can fix this mess, but you being here for me makes a difference. Don't think for a second that it doesn't."

She smiled and steered me over to the closest bed and pulled the covers down. "In you go, get comfortable 'cause there a ton of Spankovision movies we can watch."

I surprised myself by giggling in response. We'd called the movie rentals at hotels Spankovision ever since we'd discovered that they had porn during a road trip with her parents in middle school. Of course we'd rented one and were stunned by what we'd seen. We were even more surprised the next morning when we were asked about the movie we'd watched the night before. Our blushes must have given us away, and her brothers had teased us mercilessly the rest of the trip about the whole thing. The easiest way to stop the guys when they were on a roll was to join in and make fun of ourselves too. If you can't beat 'em, join 'em. Or something like that.

Aubrey beamed at me, enjoying my reaction to the memory. "Since I get first pick, we're doing a girlie movie. I'm sure I'll end up watching enough of your action flicks later to make up for it. Maybe we'll get lucky and my movie will even put you to sleep."

I nodded tiredly and hugged one of the pillows to my body as the movie started. I tried my best to stop thinking about what had happened with Drake and enjoy the movie, but it was so hard to do. A love story was a really bad idea. As I watched the couple on screen fall in love, I couldn't stop myself from wishing life were as easy as it seemed in the movie. Boy meets girl, boy loses girl, boy gets girl back. Would our story have a happy ending too? I just didn't see how it was possible without any trust. And thinking that those awful lies about me were true showed that Drake didn't really trust me, let alone really know me at all.

Thoughts swirling round and round in my head, I closed my eyes in an effort to block everything out. It must have worked better than I'd planned since I woke up several hours later when the hotel door slammed shut, pulling me from a deep sleep. The sound startled me and I jumped out of bed.

"Oops, sorry!" Aubrey apologized. She was standing there with her hands full of grocery store bags and a drink carrier from Dairy Queen. "I thought I could catch the door with my foot, but I missed."

I pulled the drinks from her hands. "You brought me my favorite?" I asked.

"Yeah. I figured you wouldn't really be hungry, and Dairy Queen banana milkshakes always worked for your dad when you were sick."

"You are so sweet. Thank you!" I exclaimed while unwrapping a straw. There was something comforting about drinking it, and I needed all the comfort I could get right about now.

"I got enough supplies to last us a couple days," she said, pulling a bunch of my favorite junk food from the bags along with a big bottle of Three Olives vodka. "And if you get your appetite back, we can always order pizza, too."

I glanced at the dresser and realized she'd left her phone here while she was out. "You didn't bring your phone with you? That's not safe, Aubrey! What if you'd had car trouble?"

"Oh please. I know everyone in town. If I'd had any problems, someone was bound to find me, or I could have walked to the closest house and called for help. It's no biggie. Besides, I was only gone for like thirty minutes."

I looked at the bags and back at Aubrey. "Thirty minutes? The store is only a couple blocks away, and Dairy Queen is right next door."

She looked at me sheepishly. "Well, I wanted to run back to the dorm to grab a couple things, but I changed my mind when I got there."

"Why?" I asked, confused by her answer. "What could have possibly made you decide not to run inside after driving back to campus?"

"I saw Drake's car sitting outside the dorm, so I didn't pull into the parking lot. I didn't want to run into him, and I certainly didn't want him to see me because then he'd want to know where you were."

"Drake was there?" I shrieked, stunned. Just hearing his name hurt.

"Yes. Parked right at the curb with the engine running."

I sat back down on the bed and glanced at my phone. "That means he wants to talk to me."

Aubrey picked up my phone, tossed it into her purse, and zipped it shut. "It won't hurt him to wait for you. Maybe it will give him time to understand how badly he hurt you. And you need some time to decide what you want to say to him. I'm not giving you this back until Sunday morning. So don't even try to convince me otherwise. I see that look on your face. No caving yet. If you guys stay together, you need to make sure he understands that you won't put up with crap like this. You've heard my mom's advice on relationships almost as often as I have."

"Start as you mean to go on," we said in unison, wagging our fingers at each other just like her mom did whenever she said the same thing.

"You're right. I don't even know what he could say that would make his accusations forgivable, but I can't talk to him until I figure out what I want to do. God, Aubrey… He made me fall in love with him and then he crushed me. Shattered my heart into a million pieces. How are we ever going to move on from this?"

"I'm not sure, sweetie. Let's just take it one day at a time, I guess. Tonight, don't even think about it. Let's just hang out, watch movies, and eat junk food. I even grabbed swimsuits so we can hang out in the hot tub. Don't make any decisions you'll regret until you've had time to process what happened. Okay?"

I nodded my head in agreement. "But make sure you hide that phone better because it's killing me right now not to call him, knowing that he's trying to find me."

"Girl, please. You know you aren't getting it away from me until Sunday. So don't even bother trying. And none of your puppy-dog eyes later either. A day and a half isn't going to kill you, especially after storming out the way you did. You're too much of a softie, so leave it to me to be your backbone this time around."

And she really was. We spent the rest of the night and all of the next day doing anything but talking about my relationship problems. We managed to polish off the bottle of vodka and then passed out to sleep it off. I tried a couple times to talk her into just checking my phone to see if he left any more messages, but she wouldn't hear of it. She knew me well enough to know that I wouldn't be able to resist calling him. Even while drunk, she insisted that a total communications blackout was the way to go, and she wouldn't budge an inch.

Chapter 15

SUNDAY MORNING FINALLY rolled around, and I just lay in bed, staring at the ceiling for a while after I woke up. My stomach cramped when I realized that I was going to have to face everything today. I was glad that Aubrey had made me wait since I was a lot calmer than I had been on Friday. And stronger, too.

I rolled over to find Aubrey watching me from the other bed. She'd spent the whole weekend showing me exactly why we were best friends, dropping everything to help me through this mess. I was so lucky to have her in my life.

"Thank you, Aubrey," I whispered in a heartfelt tone.

"Dude, save the gratitude. You know you're going to repay the favor someday," she teased, lightening the mood. "Hell, the way I go through guys, I'm due for someone to stomp on my heart soon as payback. Karma's a bitch."

I chuckled as I looked at the clock before locking my eyes onto hers. "It's time," I said, taking a deep breath to calm my nerves. I held out my hand, knowing she'd understand what I meant.

She shook her head at me as she got out of bed and went to grab the phones. "Nope, let me check mine first. I want to make sure that there isn't some horrible news waiting for you before I hand your phone over to you. Go hop in the shower and get dressed. If we're going to leave our little hideaway, you might as well get ready first."

"I don't know if I can wait," I protested.

"Well, that's just too damn bad. You need to be ready for anything, and the only way that's going to happen is if you're showered and dressed before you check all the messages I am sure are waiting for you on this," she said, waving my phone at me. "Now run along and make yourself presentable or I'm not giving it back."

"Argh! Fine," I grumbled as I stomped into the bathroom. It pained me to admit that she did have a point. If there was bad news, then I would be more prepared to face it after I'd gotten ready for the day. The last thing I wanted to do was confront Drake looking like crap. If things were going to end between us, I wanted to at least look good enough that he'd regret losing me for being such an ass.

I took the quickest shower in history, ready to just get this over with. I could hear Aubrey's voice through the bathroom door and threw on a robe so I could find out who she was talking to. I found her sitting on the bed, phone pressed to her ear with her hand over her mouth, looking stunned.

"Jackson, she just finished her shower. Can I call you back?" she asked. After listening to him for a couple minutes, she replied by saying, "Yeah, I hear what you're saying, and I'll let her know."

"What?" I asked as she ended the call.

"Sit down," she instructed. She must have seen the fear in my eyes because she moved quickly to reassure me. "No, it's not bad. I'm pretty sure you're going to be relieved to hear what Jackson had to tell me."

I flopped down onto the bed and waited for her to continue.

"First with the not-so-great news. Jackson and Drake were in a fight. Neither of them is really hurt, but things got physical between them after you left on Friday. Drake tried to get past Jackson to get to you, and Jackson stopped him long enough for you to get away."

"And they're both okay?" I asked.

"Yeah, just some cuts and bruises. Jackson said Drake wasn't really fighting back. He just kept trying to get to the door. My brother was really pissed, so Drake got most of the damage."

"What else did Jackson have to say?"

"Well, that's where the good news comes in. You know that my brother would do just about anything to protect you from being hurt, right?" she asked.

"Yes, he proved that after everything happened with Brad."

"Exactly. He wouldn't let Brad anywhere close to you after that douche fucked things up. But he told me that he thinks you need to hear Drake out."

"What?" I exclaimed. "How did they go from fighting to Jackson being on Drake's side?"

"You know he's on your side, just like I am. He didn't give me a whole lot of details because he said it would be best if you talked to Drake to hear it from him instead of one of us. But the fact that he thinks you should see Drake at all says a lot to me."

"And where is Drake now?" I asked.

"Jackson said he's still waiting at the dorm for you to come back. He hasn't left since he got there, only about half an hour after I left to meet you."

"But that was two whole days ago!"

"I know. Jackson tried talking him into going back to the frat house, but Drake told him he wasn't leaving unless it was because he knew where you were so he could go get you. Jackson has been bringing him food, and Faith took pity on him and let him use our bathroom. She told Jackson that he'd stopped to check our room each time he came inside and just stared at your bed with a sad look on his face."

"And Jackson wouldn't even give you a hint at why he thinks I should talk to Drake?" I asked, unsure what to think of this turn of events.

"He just said that, while he didn't agree with the way Drake handled the situation, he did understand why he flew off the handle after talking to him. Judging by the number of messages I had from Jackson, Faith, and Natalie, I've gotta admit that I'm really curious to know what he said because it had to have been pretty convincing for everyone to be so persistent in trying to find us. And that's not including how many times Drake called me and sent text messages, practically begging me to have you call him. I can only imagine how many messages you have from him," she said as she handed me my phone.

I powered it up and opened up my text message notification message first. Holy shit, Drake had sent me nearly one hundred messages in two days. I had about a dozen from Jackson and a few from Natalie and Faith each. There were also several from my Dad, which I opened first. He had gotten my message on Friday and just wanted to let me know he was thinking of me. By the time I got to his last message, he was worried because Drake had called him to ask if he knew where I was. It was from last night, and he wanted me to call him ASAP.

I looked up at Aubrey, who was watching me with concern in her pretty blue eyes. "My dad knows something's up. Drake called him last night."

"Uh-oh. You better call him first so he knows you're okay then."

I nodded in agreement and decided I'd better do it now before I freaked out from reading all of Drake's messages. I dialed his number and waited for him to answer.

"Alexa, honey, is everything okay?" he asked worriedly.

"Hi, Daddy. I'm okay," I answered.

"What's going on? Why doesn't Drake know where you are?"

"We had a fight, and I've been with Aubrey while I tried to figure things out. I'm sorry he bothered you with this," I apologized.

"That's what dads are for, to be bothered with things like this. Why didn't you tell me about the fight? I've been worried sick all night, wondering what was going on."

"I'm really sorry, Dad. I sent you a message right before I turned my phone off. I just needed some time to get my head straight before I figured out what to do."

"Alexa Marie, you can't run away like that without me knowing where you are. It just isn't safe," he chastised.

"I was with Aubrey the whole time, perfectly safe at a hotel. I didn't even leave the room once. And I had no idea Drake would call you, making you worry about me. I absolutely would have told you more if I had known he'd do that."

"Just promise me you won't ever do something like that again, not without telling me where you are, okay?" he asked.

"I promise, Dad. I should have thought to let you know where Aubrey and I went, and I won't ever make the same mistake again," I swore to him.

"Now, what's going on with you and Drake? Do you need me to come home early? I can try to find someone to come up here and pilot for me," he offered.

"I really love you for that, Dad, but you don't need to come back

148

now. I haven't talked to Drake yet, but I'm going to call him now. I just wanted to talk to you first to make sure you knew I was alright."

"Okay, honey. I don't need any details, but I hope everything goes well when you talk. Between you hiding away all weekend and the way he sounded on the phone, I'm guessing the fight was a real doozy."

"It was, Dad, but Jackson has talked to Drake and told Aubrey that I should give him a chance to explain. That has to be a good sign, right?" I asked hopefully.

He was silent for a moment before answering. "Yes, Alexa. If Jackson is urging you to talk to Drake, then that's definitely a good sign. Will you send me a text to let me know how things go?"

"Sure. I'm going to call Drake now. Love you."

"Love you, too. Talk to you later," he said before disconnecting the call. I looked down at the phone in my hands, scared to open the messages Drake had left me.

"It will be okay, Lex," Aubrey encouraged me. She came over, sat down next to me, and gripped my free hand.

I started with the first message and slowly worked my way through the list. They began fairly angry, with him asking me where the hell I went and telling me that this wasn't over yet. Around the time Jackson must have talked to him, the tone change abruptly to asking me to please call him back and apologizing for his behavior. Yesterday's messages practically begged me to at least let him know that I was safe so he wouldn't worry. He told me that he was going crazy not knowing where to find me and that he knew he'd hurt me. Tears rolled down my cheeks as I realized that the depth of his pain matched mine.

The second-to-last was a message from about thirty minutes ago, telling me that if he didn't hear from me this morning he was going to call the police to file a missing persons report. He'd already asked and they'd told them he had to wait forty-eight hours. The last message came through as I was reading the rest, and I was bawling by the time I finished reading them all.

Drake: Baby, please come home. Jackson told me he finally talked to Aubrey & you're safe. I get that you're mad and hurt,

but please come back so I can see you. I know I fucked up big time, and you don't owe me anything. If you don't want to talk to me yet, I promise to leave. I just need to see you with my own eyes.

It was the longest text he'd ever written me. I had several voice-mail messages from him as well, and I played them all in succession, their tone echoing the texts I'd already read. My box was full by Saturday afternoon, which must be why he'd sent so many messages. Once I was done, I looked at Aubrey and realized she was crying too.

"You ready for this?" she asked.

"Not really, but it's not like I can feel any worse after talking to him than I do right now," I said as I dialed the number and held the phone to my ear.

"Alexa," he breathed into the phone after picking up before the first ring was even done. He didn't say anything else. He just waited for me to pull myself together so I could speak.

"Drake, I need to see you, too," I choked out in a raspy voice, my throat sore from all the crying I had done.

I heard him heave a big sigh on the other end of the phone. "Where are you? I'll come to you right now."

"I'm at the Holiday Inn, but I can have Aubrey bring me back," I protested.

I could hear tires squealing in the background. "No, I'm already on the way. Don't go anywhere. I'll be there as fast as I can."

"Okay," I agreed. "I'll text you the room number."

When the call ended and I'd sent him the text, I turned to Aubrey. "Drake is on his way so we can talk."

"Do you want me to stay? If I leave, you won't have a car here in case your talk with him doesn't go well," she warned.

"Go ahead. I can always call you if I need a ride."

"Are you sure? I can hang out downstairs just in case," she offered.

"I'm not sure about anything right now, Aubrey," I admitted. "The only thing I know for certain is that I need to find out what happened. Why Drake would believe that about me."

"I don't feel right leaving you alone yet. I'll pack up the car, make sure Drake shows up like he said he would, and then I'll wait until you text me that it's okay for me to leave. Okay?"

"Yeah, that's probably for the best. If you don't want to be here when he gets here, then you better move fast because he didn't give me a chance to say much before he was already on his way. You've only got a couple minutes left."

"Then it's a good thing I packed light," she said as she threw our stuff back into her bag. "Don't forget to let me know if you need me to come up or if you want me to go. If I don't hear from you in thirty minutes, I'm coming back up."

I gave her a quick hug and ran into the bathroom to make sure I looked decent. I didn't really. Two days spent agonizing over what I thought was the end of our relationship, crying, and having nightmares that kept waking me up didn't leave me looking my best. The shower helped a lot, but nothing was going to get rid of the red-rimmed eyes and dark circles. My hands trembled as I played with my hair. I was so nervous about what would happen next.

After a couple minutes, there was a knock on the door. I went to answer, and there he was. He looked as tired as I felt. He had a black eye and a puffy, bruised lip from his fight with Jackson. I wanted to reach out and hug him close, but I stood there with my arms wrapped around myself instead. I was unsure of how to act because everything seemed so awkward. I took a step backwards to let him inside the room. He grabbed one of my hands as he walked past and pulled me along with him. We sat down on the edge of the bed and just looked at each other for a couple minutes. Drake hadn't let go of my hand and couldn't seem to look away from me.

"Why, Drake? What could I possibly have done to deserve your accusation?" I finally asked.

He looked down at our hands and shook his head. "Fuck, Alexa. This wasn't your fault. I never should have yelled at you the way I did. Don't talk like that."

I pulled my hands away and folded them in my lap. "If that's true, then what the hell happened?"

He clenched the hand I'd let go of into a fist and stared me in the eyes, like he was willing me to listen to him. "I woke up Friday morning to a phone call from my dad. He had some questions for me. Questions about you. Concerns about how you were paying for school based on a rumor my mom had heard."

"What?" I gasped. "Your parents think that I'm prostituting myself to pay for school? Where in the world would they get an idea like that?"

"I promise that I'll get to that part in a minute, but I want you to understand why I listened to the story at all. If it had been anyone but my dad, I swear to you that I wouldn't have considered for a second that it could be true. But he'd asked the security consultant at his company to run a quick check on your dad's finances before he called me. And the guy told him there were some red flags, money coming in more quickly than ever before starting this past summer. My dad should have waited for more information before calling me, but he was concerned. Hell, I should have asked more questions, but I was crushed by the idea that it could be true."

"Your dad had mine investigated?" I asked. "What the hell?"

"I know it sounds bad, and I've already had it out with my dad after I talked to Jackson. He feels horrible about the trouble he caused, and he wants to apologize to both you and your dad. We both handled this badly, in part because neither of us knew that the source of the bad information was Sasha."

"Sasha? You're going to sit there and blame this on her?" I asked in a disbelieving tone of voice.

"That's not what I'm saying. Most of this was my doing. If I had just waited instead of flying off the handle, things wouldn't have gone down the way they did. That's on me, and I learned my lesson when I couldn't reach you to apologize and explain for two fucking days. Trust me, it's not a mistake I'm gonna repeat ever again."

"I still don't understand. What happened exactly and how was Sasha involved?"

"I haven't talked to her about it, but Jackson and I think we figured out what happened after talking to my mom. She got a call a few days ago from Sasha's mom, who told her that she was worried about how quickly our relationship moved and if I knew what I was getting into with you. They may be best friends, but my mom wasn't going to listen to her bad-mouth you without cause. And that's when she dropped the bombshell that started the ball rolling on this mess.

She told my mom that there was a rumor going around the school that you were selling sex to pay for college. She didn't have any details, but she thought my mom should know because where there's smoke there's usually a fire. Sasha had approached her mom and supposedly asked for advice on whether or not to ask me if I'd heard the rumor yet or not."

"Yeah, right. Like she needs advice to figure out a way to try to tear me down with you," I scoffed, finding the idea ridiculous.

"I think Sasha knew exactly what she was doing. She had to know that her mom would come to mine with her concerns and eventually it would filter down to me. This way, it wasn't coming from her and I would be more likely to listen. Of course my mom mentioned the conversation to my dad, and he thought it was too risky not to check into the story. She played all of us perfectly, and it almost worked."

"Not almost. It did work. You believed the rumor," I said accusingly.

"Baby, no. I didn't, not really. If I had waited at all before confronting you, I never would have handled it the way I did. I know that's not the type of person you are. There isn't a chance in hell that you would ever do that, but I let my jealousy at the thought of anyone else getting close to you fuck with my head. I swear to God that I would have realized what the hell I was saying if you had just stayed a little longer and talked to me."

"No way! Why would I stay and listen to that bullshit? You would never put up with that kind of crap from me, but you expect me to do it?" I argued.

He shook his head and raised his hands in the air in a gesture of mock surrender. "That's not what I'm saying. I get why you left. I don't blame you for it, but we have to figure out this talking thing. I refuse to lose you over some stupid story that I shouldn't have listened to in the first place."

"Then why did you listen?"

"Because it was my dad. How could I not listen to him, even just a little? I didn't know about the flights you offered. What the hell was I supposed to think?" he asked, frustrated, as he stood and started to pace the floor. "I wasn't even thinking, not really. It wasn't until you were gone and Jackson nailed me with a punch that I started to think clearly. He knocked some sense back into me, and I tried to find you to explain even though I was still a little pissed off. We needed to talk, but you were gone. Disappeared into thin air. You wouldn't answer my calls or texts—nothing. I still couldn't figure out what the fuck was going on, and then Jackson found me outside your dorm. He calmed down and wanted to know what happened. So I told him, and his reaction was to laugh his ass off. I swear to God, I almost killed him right then and there. I couldn't figure out what the hell was so funny until he told me about your Mile High Club flights."

"That's what this was about? My tours?"

"Yeah, it's the only thing that makes sense. Jackson told me that Aubrey likes to tease you about them sometimes. We figure Sasha overheard something and that's what she told her mom about. Some stupid inside joke she didn't understand that got all twisted up by the time my dad called me." He knelt down on the floor in front of me. "Please try to understand why I freaked out. You know how I am about you. I don't even like other guys looking at you. The idea of someone touching what's mine... I lost it."

I couldn't stop myself from reaching out to brush his hair from his forehead. As soon as my fingers touched him, he leaned forward to wrap his arms around me and rested his head in my lap. It felt so good to have him close to me again. My phone beeped, and I realized that it was Aubrey checking to make sure I was okay. "Will you take me back to campus when we're done talking?" I asked.

He squeezed me even tighter. "I'll take you anywhere you want to go. Just don't leave yet."

I tapped out a quick reply to Aubrey, letting her know she could leave. "Okay."

He sat back down on the floor and looked up at me with so much love in his eyes that tears started to leak from my eyes again. I hated the distance between us right now.

"After Jackson and I talked, I called my dad back to explain, but he had already figured it out. He pulled up your dad's website and saw the link for the Mile High Club. He had tried calling me to tell me what he'd found, but I wasn't picking up because we had already fought. I was focused on finding you and getting you to talk to me."

I was horrified by the idea of his parents knowing about the flights. "Your parents must think I'm horrible," I cried out.

"No, baby. My dad thinks you're brilliant. He's a businessman, and there's nothing he respects more than good business decisions. When he finally got me on the phone, he raved about your idea and how you should franchise it."

"And your mom?" I asked. I hadn't gotten to know his dad very well yet, but I really liked his mom. I hoped she wasn't disappointed in me.

He chuckled under his breath at my question, his eyes twinkling with humor again. "My mom told me that if it wasn't so damn awkward to think about you flying the plane she'd book one of the flights herself so she and dad could join the club."

I giggled at the thought of his mom as one of my customers. "Really?"

"Yes, really. She also told me that I'm an idiot if I let you get away from me because we're perfect for each other."

I beamed down at him, happy that his parents still approved of me. "Are you?" I asked.

He looked confused by my question. "Am I an idiot?"

"Are you going to let me get away?" I asked.

A look of such relief crossed his face. "Do you want me to?" he asked.

"No, I really don't," I sobbed out, starting to cry as a rush of emotions hit me.

Drake held me close as I broke down. "Fuck, Alexa. I'm sorry I messed up. I never meant to hurt you like this. You've gotta know that, baby."

I nodded my head and burrowed even closer to him. "I'm sorry, too. I shouldn't have stormed out the way I did. It just hurt so much to think that you'd really believe those things about me."

He lay back onto the bed, cradling me against his chest. "No, you were right to leave. I don't want you to take shit from anyone, not even me. Wish I didn't have to lose two days with you to learn that lesson, but it's true just the same."

"I should have at least told you about the Mile High Club stuff. Maybe if you had known, this wouldn't have happened," I admitted.

"Why didn't you tell me before?"

"I was kind of embarrassed. They really aren't as bad as they sound. Most of my customers are bored wives looking to spice up their marriages. I don't hear or see a thing. To me, it's just more time up in the air. And they pay really well for it, too. But how do I bring it up in conversation? 'Oh, by the way, I've got to be at the airport early tonight because my sightseeing tour wants to make sure they have plenty of time to screw'?"

Drake laughed at my crass question. "You had more than three months to figure it out. Gotta admit I didn't like that Jackson had to explain to me what was going on in your life. I'm your boyfriend, Alexa. There shouldn't be secrets like that between us. Especially not stupid shit. You've got to fucking know that I would understand about this."

"I'm sorry," I whispered. "I hate that my avoiding telling you about the flights caused this."

"No more secrets," he growled.

"None. I promise. I've learned my lesson, too. I don't ever want to go through something like this again," I promised.

Drake kissed my temple softly at my words. "Neither do I. I missed you so damn much," he rasped out.

His sexy tone sent tingles up my spine. Sitting here, whispering in bed, made me feel so connected to him. It was just so intimate. His kisses moved across my cheek before he nipped at my lips. He pulled my bottom lip down with his teeth, and I gasped in response. His tongue swept inside, devouring me. Drake held me in place for our kiss, his hands clenched tightly in my hair. Once we were both gasping for air, one of his hands cupped my ass. He pulled me over on top of him, my sex resting right over his cock. Pressed together like that, I couldn't stop myself from grinding my pelvis against his.

"Please, Drake. I need you now. It's been too long," I begged.

"Fuck," he groaned as he clawed at the front of his jeans to open them. He pushed them down to his knees, and his erect cock sprang free. In a flash, I felt him rip my yoga pants down my legs before he pulled my panties to the side. I was dripping wet, and it made it easy for him to slide up inside of me as he pulled me down onto him. I gripped his chest and pushed down until he was buried deep. Holding still, I savored the feel of him.

"Baby, I need you to move," he moaned.

I rode him, moving slowly at first. I rotated my hips in full circles, rubbing my clit against his pelvic bone at the end of each one. After about a dozen strokes, he gripped my hips in his hands and pushed up. Sinking even farther inside, he angled his cock and found a spot that drove me wild with need. He hammered into me, hitting the same spot over and over again, pushing me to the edge. One hand slipped from my hip, and his thumb found my clit and rubbed. The added touch was too much, and I came.

My body trembled as he continued to pound into me. When my climax was done, he flipped me onto my stomach and pulled me up onto my hands and knees. I felt his hot breath on my ass before he started to eat me from behind. He slid his stiffened tongue into my pussy and fucked me with it for a few strokes. I moaned in response, and his hands gripped my hips harder. He pulled his tongue out and licked back and forth, slashing it around my engorged clit. Once I was dripping with need again, he got to his knees behind me and thrust inside.

"Drake!" I screamed as I clawed at the sheets.

"Fuck, baby. You're so tight," he groaned. He slid in and out of me with slow strokes that teased. His hands held my hips in place so I couldn't push back onto him.

"Please, Drake," I begged. I was so close to the edge again, but I needed more from him in this position.

"Please what, Alexa?" he taunted me as he continued his relentless pace.

"Give me more. Please, I need it. I need to come so badly," I moaned as I tried desperately to thrust my hips to force him deeper inside.

"Oh, you're gonna come again and again, baby. Help me get you there this time. Play with your clit," he demanded.

I released the sheet that was gripped in my hand and reached down my body to tweak my clit. I slipped my fingers around his cock to gather some moisture to make it feel even better. He groaned at the contact and pounded into me hard. Tugging at my clit, I came around his cock, my legs quivering underneath me. He pushed me to my back and drove back inside with my legs wrapped around his hips.

He thrust in and out, my pussy clamped on him as he tried to make up for lost time.

Sweat dripped from Drake's face as he stared into my eyes. "I need to watch you fly apart for me again," he groaned.

He pumped like a madman, and I dug my nails into his ass. His eyes darkened even further, his deep feelings for me shining from them. "I love you," I whispered, not able to hold the words back any longer.

My words were his undoing. "Alexa, shit," he groaned as he emptied inside of me. His orgasm triggered another for me, its waves rolling over my body. I closed my eyes as my body shuddered. "Baby, open your eyes and look at me."

My lids opened languidly, sleepy from the lack of good sleep the last couple days and coming three times in a row. "Mmmmm," I murmured as I smiled up at him.

"Love you too, baby," he whispered as he leaned down to kiss me again. "So fucking much," he continued as I drifted off to sleep. Drake curled around me and closed his eyes.

I woke up a couple hours later and stretched. I was safely tucked into Drake's arms and rolled in them to face him. He looked at me with sleepy eyes. "Hey," I whispered.

He kissed me lightly. "How did you sleep?" he asked.

"Great! I really needed that. No nightmares about never being with you again. Waking up in your arms," I sighed.

"Only good dreams from now on, Alexa," he said as he rolled on top of me. "I love you so much, baby. I should have told you sooner."

I opened my legs and rolled my hips against him. "Me too. I was so stupid to not see it sooner."

He slipped the tip of his hardness inside and held still above me. "Alexa, no. Don't ever say that. You're the best thing that ever happened to me."

"Sorry," I sighed, wiggling my hips to try to move him farther into my body.

He kissed me deeply and took a few slow strokes. "Now we don't have to hold back anymore. I can love you the way I wanted to from the start."

I tangled my fingers into his hair and kissed him back. "Thank you," I whispered as I nuzzled his neck.

"For what, baby?"

"For saving me from the loneliness. For opening my eyes. For loving me."

He touched his forehead to mine. "Let me love you, baby. I need to show you how you make me feel," he moaned.

He propped himself on his elbows and looked deeply into my eyes. I wrapped my legs around his waist, keeping him close. "I love you, Drake."

He continued to thrust slowly, in and out. He kept his eyes open, as though he didn't want to miss a moment of us together. I gasped, my breath quickening, and tightened my arms around him. My muscles contracted around him, and I buried my head against his shoulder as I cried out in release. He took several more long strokes into me before he came, calling my name. I clung tightly to him, almost afraid to let go and find this was all a dream.

We eventually made it into the shower, washing each other slowly. We held each other under the pulsing water, kissing often. It was like a weight had been lifted now that our pent-up emotions were free and out in the open. As much as I regretted our fight and walking away, even for the short time it took to clear my head, our bond was now stronger than ever before.

epilogue

Drake

I COULDN'T STOP staring at Alexa as she lay sleeping in bed next to me. Losing her, even for one weekend, had ripped my heart out of my chest. Before our fight, I thought I'd known how much she meant to me. Making her so angry and upset that she'd stormed away and refused to speak to me showed me that I'd had no fucking clue how important she was.

The moment I first saw her on campus, I should have chased after her and not wasted a single minute. I knew—I fucking knew right away that she would change my life. If I had just gone after her right away, then I wouldn't have been such a dick when we finally met. I would have known that she looked at Jackson like a brother, even if his feelings for her went deeper than that. She had no fucking clue the way guys looked at her, how Jackson looked at her. She just went about her day, wrapped up in whatever thoughts were rolling around her head. Thank fuck that I was able to break in there and make her see me.

When my dad called me to ask about Alexa's job and how she was paying for school, I'd been blown away by the rumor he had heard. I should have asked him for more details, but my mind had been filled with images of other guys touching my girl. I just couldn't think straight. I lost my temper and almost messed up so badly that I couldn't ever get her back. I didn't know what I would have done if Jackson hadn't made me see what an ass I was being. Once I'd been thinking clearly again, I knew there wasn't a chance in hell she would ever do something like that.

When I called my dad back and realized that Sasha had caused all of this, I'd wanted to wring her neck. Jackson had promised that he'd make sure she didn't interfere in our relationship again. He told me to focus on what was important—making Alexa understand that I never would have believed a word if it hadn't been my own father who had called me. I went crazy not knowing where she was, and Jackson pulled through for me by hunting his sister down and convincing her to talk Alexa into hearing me out. He proved to me that he wanted what was best for Alexa, and I owed him a debt that I could never repay.

I'd spent the last month trying to prove to her that she'd made the right decision in taking me back. I couldn't say that I was very excited by the whole Mile High Club flight thing since people had sex right behind her while she flew the plane, but I had a couple custom t-shirts made for us as one of her Christmas presents to show my support. She got a kick out of them and wore hers to bed most nights. I understood why she hadn't told me about the flights earlier, and after thinking the worst, it was a relief to learn that an inside joke about them was what Sasha had overheard and used to try to drive a wedge between us. I wasn't going to let anything else come between us again.

I pulled open the drawer in the nightstand next to the bed. Reaching inside, I pulled out a small blue box. I peeked back at Alexa to make sure she was still sleeping soundly. I knew she wasn't ready for this yet. My hands trembled as I popped the box open. My last trip back home, this damn ring fucking screamed to me from the jewelry store window. It was perfect for Alexa. The four carat diamond twinkled in the light from the lamp. I couldn't wait to see it on her finger and know that she would be mine forever.

I knew my parents were going to freak the fuck out when we got engaged. My dad had dreams for me that didn't include my getting married young. But he'd understand when I explained that she was as important to me as mom was to him. He worshipped the ground she walked on. No fucking way he wouldn't stand behind me on this when I made him understand that. And if I had to resort to a guilt trip and remind him that he'd almost destroyed my relationship with his meddling, then so be it. I'd do what needed to be done to make sure that Alexa stayed by my side.

I heard the sheets rustle as she rolled over, and I put the ring back in the drawer. As I closed it, her hand reached out for me. I rolled back towards her and pulled her into my arms. Her eyes were still closed, with dark smudges underneath them. I wore her the fuck out last night. It was like I was trying to make up for lost time—I couldn't get enough of her.

As she slept in my arms, she let out a small sigh and her lips tilted in a smile. She must be dreaming of me then. I kissed her cheek lightly so I didn't wake her and closed my eyes to catch a quick nap before she woke up. Wouldn't do for me to be tired later on. I had her all to myself for the day, and I intended to make the most of it. We were going to start the new year off the right way—together.

HIT THE WALL

Jackson

I COULDN'T BELIEVE that I had to deal with this bullshit. It was bad enough that I had to watch Lex fall for Drake, but now I had to go talk to Sasha about the crap she'd pulled to fuck with their relationship. I could have just kept my mouth shut, and not said anything to Drake about Lex's job. I could have just enjoyed the fuck out of punching him and then waited to see if they'd stay broken up. But no, I couldn't stand to know that she was hurting when I could do something to fix it.

I'd grown up with Lex in my life, always thinking of her as my other little sister. She and Aubrey were attached at the hip, and she spent almost as much time at our house as she did her dad's. Then she'd hit her teens and filled out. I couldn't help but notice her new tits, and she started to show up in my spank bank. It freaked me out the first time I thought of her while jacking off in the shower, but I figured it was normal and shrugged it off. She was dating Brad, and there were plenty of girls in high school for me to mess around with.

The night I caught Brad cheating on her changed everything. I held her in my arms as she fell apart, and I realized I wanted her for my own. It was the absolute worst fucking timing to figure out that I didn't love her like a sister. I just loved her.

She needed time to get over Brad and what he did. She wasn't ready for a boyfriend, and I couldn't just play with her. My mom would kill me if I didn't treat Lex right. I knew that when we got together that would be it. So I enjoyed the girls in college while I waited. Tried new things and discovered I like my sex hard and rough. I waited some more so I could get it out of my system before going to her. I put it off so long that Drake swooped in and stole her right out from underneath my nose.

I knew the second I saw them together that I had waited too long. He wanted her, and I couldn't blame him. She was hot. Lots of guys wanted her. It was the way she looked at him that got to me. Her eyes lit up any time he was near, and she'd get this look on her face. Like he was the only thing she could see. I tried to tell myself it was only a fling and that it was a good sign. She was ready for a relationship again. I just had to wait until Drake messed up, and then I could finally have Lex. But when it came down to it, I just couldn't do it. She loved him, and he made her happy. More than anything, I wanted her to be happy.

When Drake calmed down and listened to me, the look of horror on his face told me he loved her, too. My worst fear was confirmed when he refused to budge from her dorm, unwilling to go anywhere until he could find Lex. By the time Aubrey finally answered her phone, I felt sorry for the guy. He was a total wreck knowing how much he had hurt her. If she forgave him, he wasn't ever going to let her go. So I had to do it.

Now here I am, on my way to find Sasha to make sure she doesn't interfere in their relationship again. Talk about an awkward conversation. I had to talk to a chick that I banged the fuck out of last year. About not messing with the girl that I'm in love with and her boyfriend. The situation is so fucked up that I couldn't make this shit up if I tried.

BONUS
Drake POV:
Before Alexa

CHANGING SCHOOLS YOUR junior year would normally suck ass, but the transfer to Blythe College was pretty seamless for me. I'd met the rugby guys over the summer, so I already knew people on campus who were chill. And they had a Sigma Chi chapter that was happy to have a fellow brother from another school, so I didn't have to stay in the dorms. Add in a whole new school full of women I'd never dated and this seemed like a pretty great deal to me. It would be like shooting fish in a barrel from what I could tell.

Or at least that had been the plan until I saw Alexa. I was with my new frat brothers, scoping out chicks on campus, and the next thing I knew, I couldn't see anything but her. I literally stopped mid-stride to stare. Dead in my tracks. I tore my eyes away when one of my buddies asked me what was wrong, and she was gone by the time my head swiveled back in her direction. Like I had imagined her or something.

I wasn't even sure what it was about her that had drawn my attention so strongly. I'd never had something happen to me like that before, no matter how hot a chick was. We were surrounded by girls dressed in way less clothes than she was. Girls who were practically begging for attention from us. That's why we were wandering around campus for fuck's sake—so we could check out the fresh meat. Yet I suddenly found myself searching for the one with long brown hair who clearly didn't give a damn based on the jeans, t-shirt, and flip-flops she had been wearing.

Over the next couple of weeks, I felt like I'd been cursed with horrible timing. I'd catch a glimpse of her here and there, but I never got the chance to talk to her. I wasn't a shy guy—not by any stretch of the imagination. That wasn't the problem. I just needed an opening so I could fucking go up to her. I swear to God, every single time I saw her again, there was some chick hanging on me, trying to get my attention. Not exactly the way I wanted to meet this girl.

From what I'd seen of her so far, I figured she'd shoot me down just as easily as she'd talk to me. I never really saw any guys around her, which was fucking insane considering how hot she was. It was a good thing I didn't because I wasn't sure what I'd do if I saw some guy all over her. I hadn't even spoken a single word to her, but I already knew that shit would piss me off big time.

I knew it sounded fucking crazy. I didn't understand what the hell was going on, but I had finally run out of patience. As I was getting ready for my first frat party at my new school, I still couldn't stop thinking about her. It was pretty damn clear that I wasn't going to be able to get her out of my head any time soon. So I decided that I was going to find her on Monday and talk to her—no matter what.

And then it happened again, only worse. I was stuck in an argument with Sasha, a girl I knew from back home who seemed to think that made me her property. She hadn't been invited to the party, and I hadn't thought to add her to the list, so she was pissed at me. Yeah, our moms were best friends, so I should have probably done it, but sue me if my mind was on other things. The next thing I knew, she was bitching me out at the back door, and the girl I've been searching everywhere for walks into the kitchen with Jackson Silver.

Jackson and I had hung out a bit since I'd gotten here. He was an interesting dude, hot tempered, and liked his kink from what I'd heard around campus. Not exactly the type of guy I pictured my laid-back girl hanging out with. At least not from the way she looked around campus. She looked totally different tonight though. She was smoking hot in a purple dress that barely covered her ass, her face done up and her hair all curly down her back. And her legs. The second I scanned down, I could picture them wrapped around my hips as I drove deep inside her. With that dress, she turned me into a leg man.

My staring at her legs sure as shit pissed Sasha off, but Jackson helped me get her out the door. I couldn't stop myself from looking at Alexa as we talked, but Jackson caught on and warned me away from her.

"Fuck no, man. No way in hell are you going there," Jackson warned me while shaking his head.

I could feel my body tense up. I wanted to punch him in the face so damn much. I had been waiting weeks for my chance with this girl, and now he was going to fuck it up for me because he'd somehow managed to get there first. I felt the anger bubble up inside me at the thought of the two of them together.

Jackson reached out to grab my arm, but I backed away. I didn't trust myself not to get into it with him while she was watching us.

I turned to glare at her as Jackson kept talking. His words didn't even register with me through my red haze of anger and jealousy. I hadn't even spoken to her yet and she already had me all twisted up inside. I continued to glare at her from across the kitchen, royally pissed that she didn't feel this thing between us too. If she had, there was no way I'd be watching her ass as she and Jackson talked for a couple of minutes before heading up the stairs to his room. To his fucking room. In my frat house. How the fuck was I going to be able to stay here without doing something totally fucked up, like knocking his goddamn door down?

Fuck this shit. I headed out the door to clear my head and realized what weekend it was. My mom's birthday. A perfect excuse to get the fuck out of town, I thought as I grabbed my phone to call my dad. I was sure he'd figure a way to get me the hell out of here and back home for the party tomorrow.

BONUS Drake POV: The Dress

A S I WALKED away from the guest house, I knew I'd do whatever it took to make sure Alexa came to the party tonight. I'd already fucked up badly enough by waiting to make a move, jumping to conclusions about her and Jackson, and then being an ass to her. Repeatedly.

So I was going to grab the opportunity I'd been given this weekend to make her mine, and I was going to do it fast. I needed to wrap this shit up tight with her because there was no way in hell I was going to let more time pass. The first thing I needed to do was make sure she couldn't use the lame 'I don't have anything to wear' excuse to get out of tonight. And I knew exactly what I wanted to see her in and who could help me get this thing done.

"Hey," my little sister Drea said, answering the phone. "Are you almost here? Mom is super excited that you decided to come home this weekend for her party."

"Yeah, I'm here already, but I need your help with something."

"Ohmigod! You do?" she shrieked. "You never ask me for help with anything. Like ever."

I pulled the phone away from my ear at her response. "And you wonder why," I mumbled.

"Haha, funny. So what do you need?" she asked.

"A dress. And shoes. And I need it before tonight."

I heard her giggle in my ear. "Ummmmm, is there something you forgot to share with me? Like you've taken up cross-dressing or something?" she teased.

"It's for a girl," I muttered, knowing she was going to go crazy over this information.

"A girl? What girl? You haven't mentioned meeting anyone to me!"

"Her name's Alexa. She's staying in the guest house, but she doesn't have anything to wear to Mom's party. So I'm going to fix the problem for her. That's all," I explained.

"Uh-huh. Why do I get the feeling you aren't telling me the whole story?" she complained.

"Because you don't need to know anything else, brat. Now are you going to help me out or not?"

"Of course I'm going to help, silly. Have her come up to the house and she can take her pick from my closet and Mom's. I'm sure one of us is bound to have something she can borrow," Drea offered.

"No, it can't be just any dress and shoes. I know exactly what I want her to wear," I argued.

Drea took a deep breath before answering. "There's a girl here, staying in the guest house, who you want to come to Mom's birthday party wearing clothes you've picked out?"

When she put it like that, it sounded pretty crazy. But the truth was the truth any way you put it. "Yeah, that sounds about right. Except she can't know that I've bought her this shit. No way in hell would she accept it if she knew the truth."

I could practically hear the wheels spinning in her head as my sister processed everything I had just told her. "No problem at all. Pick me up in five minutes. We'll run into town so you can grab what you need and then switch the dress out into one of the dry cleaner's bags in my closet."

"And the shoes?" I asked.

"That's super easy. I'll just scuff up the bottoms a bit on the sidewalk so it looks like they've been worn. She'll never know the difference. But you'll owe me big time."

I chuckled. "I will, huh? I'm pretty sure I've got some markers due to me for helping you out of jams all these years, Drea."

"That's true, but if you want me to keep this a secret from your mystery girl, then you'd better tell me at least a little bit about her. Or else I'm gonna spill the beans."

I sighed deeply, not sure how to put my feelings into words. "I don't know what to say except that I haven't been able to get her out of my head ever since I saw her on campus a couple weeks ago. Shit, Drea. There's just something about her that's different."

"Well, that's enough for me. I've never seen you so flustered over a girl before. I can't wait to meet her."

"Meet me out front at my car. And you better hope she likes the dress and shoes, because she hasn't been too impressed with me so far," I warned Drea.

Bonus
Drake POV:
The Fight

"**G**ET YOUR ASS back here!" I roared as Alexa escaped out the door. Jackson pushed me back so I couldn't get past him as she raced out of the house. "Back the hell off, Jackson."

"No way, dude," he answered.

I pushed him back, knowing that if I was fast enough I could still catch her before she got too far. "Get the hell out of my way. Now."

"You aren't getting past me until I know that Alexa is gone. I may not know what the hell happened here, but I damn well can be sure that I do what she asked of me," he swore.

"This is none of your goddamn business Jackson," I argued as I tried to slide past him.

He pushed me back, blocking me from the door again. "You made it my business when you made her cry and she told me she needed to get out of here."

"She's got some explaining to do. I'm not the one who fucked up here. She is. You may think she's all innocent and shit, but that's not what I'm hearing, and I deserve to know what the hell is going on. So move. Now!" I demanded.

Jackson's eyes burned darkly as I accused Alexa of not being innocent. Before I knew what was happening, his fist slammed into my face and I flew backwards onto my ass. While we wrestled on the floor, I was trying to get away from Jackson because my fight wasn't really with him. It was with Alexa. He finally settled down when he realized I wasn't going to hit back. We sat on the floor, breathing heavily and staring at each other for a moment before he spoke.

"That's fucking bullshit. You know her better than that."

He was right. I did know her better than that. Fuck. I had royally screwed shit up her by flinging accusations at her instead of just talking to her about my dad's call. As I sat there, quietly thinking about what a mess this was, Jackson's hands dropped to his side. I had my opening to get away and took it, racing for the door. My hope was that I could still catch Alexa at her dorm. I could hear Jackson yelling behind me, but it didn't matter. I just needed to get to her. Too bad I was too late. By the time I got there, she was gone. I didn't care how long I had to wait though. I was going to be here when she came back.

I SAT BROODING in my car, waiting outside her dorm all day and night. I'd left countless voicemail messages and sent her many text messages. But I'd received radio silence from her in return. My dad had tried calling a few times, but I didn't want to talk to him yet. Not until I fixed this mess and knew what I was going to say.

Come morning, Jackson tapped on my passenger's side window before he opened the door and hopped in with me. I glared at him, still pissed off that he'd stopped me from being able to reach her in time.

"You ready to tell me what the hell happened yesterday?" he asked.

"If I do, are you going to tell me where the hell my girlfriend is?" I snapped back.

"I would if I could, but my sister turned off both of their phones before I could find out where they were going."

"Fuck!" I swore, running my hands through my hair. "She's with Aubrey? And you have no idea where they could be?"

"Nope," he answered, not sounding particularly bothered by the fact that neither of us knew how to find the girls. "So why don't you explain what's going on and we'll see if I'm willing to help you figure out where they went."

When I told him about my dad's call, my text to Alexa, and our fight, the motherfucker had the nerve to laugh in my face.

"What the hell, Jackson? There isn't anything funny about this. It's a clusterfuck."

"Dude, have you ever asked Alexa about the flights she does?"

"What do you mean?" I asked, confused at the connection between her piloting for her dad and the rumor that had gotten back to my dad.

"Fuck. I can't believe I'm going to be the one to tell you about this," he grumbled before turning in his seat to look at me. "She does mile high club flights, man. People pay her good money to go up in her plane so they can join the club."

"She does what?" I asked, unable to believe what I was hearing.

"It sounds worse than it really is. She doesn't see anything 'cause they're in the back of the plane. She doesn't even hear anything because she wears headphones the whole time. But the money is good. Damn good."

"How the hell would my dad have heard about this before me?" I wondered aloud.

"I don't know, man. She doesn't talk about it very much. Alexa's a pretty shy person, and she gets kinda embarrassed about it."

My mind was blown. I was irritated to learn that there was something big in Alexa's life that she'd shared with Jackson but not me. And I was pissed that something so simple had caused a huge misunderstanding. I grabbed my phone to call my dad.

"Drake, thank God you finally called me back."

"Hey, Dad—"

He interrupted me before I could say anything else. "I've been trying to get ahold of you all day and night. I figured out the basis for the rumor your mom heard. Your reaction didn't sit well with me, so I did a little digging on my own and found a link on her dad's website to some flights that could explain it all. For something brilliant, marketing-wise."

I chuckled darkly, realizing that, if I had waited an hour, I never would have gotten into this fight with Alexa. "Yeah, Dad. Jackson just told me about them. I had no idea. And if I didn't even know, how the hell did you hear about it?"

"Well, son, that's the other reason I've been trying to reach you. Your mom found out that I'd talked to you and freaked out a bit because it finally dawned on her that Sasha was the source of the information. She figured that maybe this was exactly what she wanted— your mom to talk to me, me to talk to you, and then you and Alexa to break up. You know that Sasha has always had a bit of a crush on you, and she's always been pretty spoiled. Thinks she deserves whatever she wants. I'm just sorry I played right into her hands on this one."

"No, Dad. This isn't your fault. It's mine. I should've held off before reacting, but I let my temper get the better of me. But don't worry. I am going to make this right with Alexa," I swore.

"Good luck, son. Let me know if there's anything we can do to help," my dad said before disconnecting the call.

Jackson had been listening into our conversation the whole time. "Sasha was behind the whole thing?" he asked.

"Yup. Sounds like it," I murmured, still stunned that something so small had blown up into a fight this big. I hadn't seen or spoken with Alexa in twenty-four hours already.

"That bitch," he muttered. "You focus on Alexa and I'll make sure Sasha understands that she better stay away from now on."

I looked across at him, amazed that he was willing to help me out with Alexa. I knew what he felt for her. It was impossible to miss, even though we had never talked about it. And I sure as shit wasn't going to say anything now.

"Thanks, man."

"No worries, dude. I'll try to get ahold of my sister. I'm not sure how easy that will be if she's in mother hen mode though. She can be crazy protective of Alexa, but I'll put in a good word for you," he said as he got out of the car.

I watched him walk away, and the next twenty-four hours went by in a blur until my phone finally rang and it was her.

Acknowledgments

Mom – Thank you for always believing in me and pushing me to make this happen. I love you!

Mickey – I am so grateful to have found an editor like you! Thanks for putting your mad editing skills to good use for me.

Melissa - Book covers are so incredibly important. Thanks for making mine fabulous!

Yolanda – You've always been there for me, and your friendship means the world to me. Thanks for being my number one cheerleader!

Crystal, Kim & Midian – My awesome beta readers! Thank you for being gentle while giving me your insight on how to make this a better story.

Love Between The Sheets Promotions – Thanks for helping me get the word out about my debut book. Natalie has been great and you all have done an amazing job pimping me! The bloggers that work with you have been so generous with their time and efforts on my behalf.

About The Author

I absolutely adore reading - always have and always will. My friends growing up used to tease me when I would trail after them, trying to read and walk at the same time. If I have downtime, odds are you will find me reading or writing.

I am the mother of two wonderful sons who have inspired me to chase my dream of being an author. I want them to learn from me that you can live your dream as long as you are willing to work for it.

When I told my mom that my new year's resolution was to self-publish a book in 2013, she pretty much told me "About time!" Connect with me online!

Facebook: http://www.facebook.com/rochellepaigeauthor

Twitter: @rochellepaige1

Goodreads: https://www.goodreads.com/author/show/7328358. Rochelle_Paige

Website: http://www.rochellepaige.com

Made in the USA
Charleston, SC
31 October 2014